P9-DMX-900

IT CAME FROM BENEATH THE SINK!

Goosebumps

IT CAME FROM BENEATH THE SINK!

R.L. STINE

AN
APPLE
PAPERBACK

SCHOLASTIC INC.
New York Toronto London Auckland Sydney

A PARACHUTE PRESS BOOK

If you purchased this book without a cover, you should be aware that this book is stolen property. It was reported as "unsold and destroyed" to the publisher, and neither the author nor the publisher has received any payment for this "stripped book."

No part of this publication may be reproduced in whole or in part, or stored in a retrieval system, or transmitted in any form or by any means, electronic, mechanical, photocopying, recording, or otherwise, without written permission of the publisher. For information regarding permission, write to Scholastic Inc., 555 Broadway, New York, NY 10012.

ISBN 0-590-48348-X

Copyright © 1995 by Parachute Press, Inc. All rights reserved. Published by Scholastic Inc. APPLE PAPERBACKS is a registered trademark of Scholastic Inc. GOOSEBUMPS is a trademark of Parachute Press, Inc.

12 11 10 9 8 7 6 5   5 6 7 8 9/9 0/0

Printed in the U.S.A.   40

First Scholastic printing, April 1995

IT CAME FROM BENEATH THE SINK!

1

Before my brother and I found the strange little creature under the sink, we were a normal happy family. In fact, I'd have to say we were very lucky.

But our luck quickly changed when we pulled the creature from its dark hiding place.

The sad, frightening story begins on the day we moved.

"Here we are, kids." Dad honked the horn happily as we rounded the corner onto Maple Lane and pulled up in front of our new house. "Ready for the big move, Kitty Kat?"

My dad is the only one who can get away with calling me Kitty Kat. My real name is Katrina (ugh!) Merton, but only the teachers call me Katrina. To everyone else I'm simply Kat.

"Definitely, Dad!" I shouted. I jumped out of the station wagon.

"Rowf! Rowf!" Killer, our cocker spaniel, barked in agreement and followed me out onto the sidewalk.

Daniel, my goofy little brother, is the one who named the dog. What a dumb name. Killer is afraid of *everything*. The only thing he kills is his rubber ball!

Daniel and I had biked past the new house plenty of times already. It's only three blocks away from where we used to live, on East Main.

But I still couldn't believe we'd be *living* here. I mean, I always thought our old house was pretty great. But this place is awesome!

Three stories high, sitting up on its own little hill, with butter-yellow shutters and at least a dozen windows. A wide porch wraps around the whole house. The front yard must be about the size of a football field.

It's not a house — it's a mansion!

Well, *practically* a mansion. Enormous — but not exactly fancy. What Mom calls "a comfortable old shoe kind of house."

Actually, today it really looked messy and old. A few of the shutters hung crookedly, the grass needed mowing, and the whole place seemed to be covered with an inch of dust.

But as Mom said, "Nothing that can't be taken care of with a good cleaning, a coat of paint, and a few bangs with the hammer."

Mom, Dad, and Daniel climbed out of the car, and we all stood staring excitedly at the house. Today, I'd finally get to see the inside!

Mom pointed to the second floor. "See that big

2

balcony?" she asked. "That's the room where your father and I will sleep. The next room over is Daniel's."

She gave my hand a little squeeze. "The little balcony — that's outside *your* room, Kat." She beamed.

My very own private porch! I leaned over and gave Mom a big hug. "I love it already," I whispered into her ear.

Naturally, Daniel started whining immediately. He's ten years old, but most of the time he acts as if he's about two.

"How come Kat's room has a balcony — and mine doesn't?" he complained. "It's not fair! I want a balcony, too!"

"Get a life, Daniel," I muttered. "Mom, tell him to be quiet. Don't I get *something* for being two years older?"

Well, almost two years older. My birthday was in four days.

"Quiet, kids," Mom ordered. "Daniel, you don't have a balcony. But you are getting something neat, too — bunk beds. So Carlo can sleep over whenever you want."

"Excellent!" Daniel shouted. Carlo is Daniel's best friend. They're always together — and always bugging me.

Daniel is okay — most of the time. But he insists on being right. Dad calls him Mr. Know-It-All.

3

And sometimes Dad calls Daniel the Human Tornado, because he runs around like a whirlwind and makes unbelievable messes.

I'm a lot more like my Dad — sort of calm and quiet. Well, usually calm. And we both have the same favorite foods — lasagna, really sour garlic pickles, and mocha-chip ice cream.

I even look like my father, tall and thin with a lot of freckles and reddish hair. I usually wear my hair in a ponytail. Dad doesn't have much hair to worry about.

Daniel looks more like my mother. Straight, light brown hair that's always falling in his eyes, and what Mom calls a "sturdy" build. (That means he's chunky.)

Today, Daniel was definitely in Human Tornado mode. He ran up onto the big green lawn and began spinning around in a circle. "It's huge," he shouted. "It's gigantic. It's . . . it's . . . it's super-house!"

He collapsed in a heap on the grass. "And this is the super-yard! Hey, Kat, look at me — I'm Super-Daniel!"

"You're super-dumb," I told him, messing up his hair with both hands.

"Hey, quit it!" Daniel yelped. He pulled out his super-soaker gun and squirted the front of my T-shirt. "You're captured," he announced. "You are my prisoner!"

4

"I don't think so," I replied, tugging on the water pistol. "Give up the gun!" I commanded. I pulled harder. "Let go!"

"Okay!" Daniel grinned. He loosened his grip so suddenly that I staggered backwards — and fell on to the sidewalk.

"What a klutz!" Daniel snickered.

I knew how to get him. I zoomed up the porch steps. "Hey, Daniel," I called, "I'm going to be first in the new house!"

"No way!" he exclaimed, scrambling up off the lawn. He hurled himself at the steps and grabbed me by the ankle. "Me first! Me first!"

That's when Dad walked up the driveway, carrying an overstuffed cardboard box with KITCHEN written on the side. Two moving men followed, hauling our big blue couch.

"Hey, stop goofing around! Mom and I really need your help today. That's why we allowed you to miss a school day," he called. "Daniel, walk Killer — and make sure he has food and water. Kat, keep an eye on Daniel.

"And Kat, clean the inside of the kitchen cabinets, okay?" Dad added. "Mom wants to start putting the dishes and pots away."

"Sure, Dad," I answered. I saw Daniel rummaging through a box on the lawn. The box was marked CARDS AND COMICS.

"Hey, where's the dog?" I yelled to him.

He shrugged.

"Daniel!" I frowned. "I don't see Killer anywhere. Where is he?"

He dropped a stack of baseball cards. "Okay, okay, I'll go find him," he mumbled. He stood up and made his way to the driveway, calling the dog's name.

As soon as he disappeared around the side of the house, I hurried to the box marked CARDS AND COMICS and checked through it. Sure enough, the little brat had stolen some of my comics.

I tucked them under my arm and walked inside to the kitchen to clean out the cabinets. One quick glance made me groan.

Cabinets filled just about every square inch of the big bright room! Sighing, I yanked paper towels and a bottle of cleaner out of the CLEANING SUPPLIES box and started scrubbing.

Spritz, rub, spritz, rub.

This could take hours!

After I finished a cabinet, I stepped back to admire my work. Then I knelt down in front of the cabinet under the sink.

But something — a squeaky noise, like the sound of a footstep on an old wooden stair — made me stop short.

What is that? I wondered, my heart beating faster.

I slowly opened the cabinet. Tried to peek inside.

I opened it a little wider. A little wider.
I heard the noise again.
My heart was pounding now.
I opened the cabinet door another inch.
And then it grabbed me.
A dark, hairy claw.
It wouldn't let go.
I screamed.

2

"Daniel! You scared me to death!" I screamed. I pounded him on the back.

Laughing his head off, my brother yanked off the stupid rat costume he had insisted on packing. "You should have seen your face!" he cried. "Know what? I'm going to start calling you Scaredy-Kat!"

"Ha-ha. Very funny," I replied, rolling my eyes. Did I mention that Daniel also thinks he's the king of practical jokes?

I suddenly remembered what my brother was *supposed* to be doing. "Dad asked you to find Killer. Where is he?"

"I didn't have to find him." Daniel snickered. "He was never lost."

"What do you mean?" I demanded.

"I stuck Killer in the basement," he said proudly. "While you were hanging around on the porch, I ran in through the side door and hid under the sink."

"You really are a big rat!" I exclaimed.

I heard a funny tap-tapping on the linoleum floor. "What's that noise?" I asked.

Daniel's mouth dropped open. "Oh, no, it's a real rat!" he shrieked. "Kat, look out! Move!"

Without thinking, I jumped on to a kitchen chair as . . . Killer came trotting into the kitchen.

Daniel let out a high-pitched laugh. "Twice on the same trick!" He was very pleased with himself.

I dove at my brother, ready to tickle him. "Prepare to die laughing!" I yelled.

"Stop! Help! No!" he gulped. "Kat, please. Stop, please. I . . . can't . . . take . . . it!"

"Give up?" I asked.

Daniel nodded. "Yes!" he half-gasped, half-laughed.

"All right," I said generously. "You can get up now."

"Thanks!" he said. "Hey, what's Killer doing over there?"

"No way. I'm not falling for another one of your tricks," I declared.

But when I glanced over, the cocker spaniel did seem very interested in something inside the sink cabinet I'd left open.

He pulled it out, then sniffed. Pushed it with his nose and gave a head-tossing growl.

That's weird, I thought. Killer *never* growls.

"What do you have there, boy?" I called to him.

The dog didn't even look up.

Sniff, sniff, sniff . . . growl.

I leaned in for a closer view.

"What is it, Kat?" Daniel asked.

"Nothing much," I answered casually. "Just an old sponge, I think."

Sniff, sniff, sniff . . . growl.

It seemed perfectly ordinary — small, round, and light brown. A little bigger than an egg.

But the sponge had Killer all excited and nervous. The dog danced around it, barking and growling.

I snatched the sponge from him to get a better look. And my sweet dog tried to bite me!

"Killer!" I yelled. "Bad boy!"

He slunk to a corner. And with an embarrassed howl, he lay his head down sadly on his paws.

I held the sponge up close to my face, to study it better.

Whoa! Wait a minute!

I suddenly understood Killer's strange behavior.

"Daniel — check it out!" I exclaimed. "Wow! I don't BELIEVE this!"

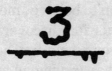

"Huh? What is it, Kat?" Daniel cried.

I stared in shock at the tiny sponge.

"Maybe my eyes are playing tricks on me," I muttered. "It's totally weird!"

"Come on, Kat," Daniel insisted. "What is it?"

I studied the sponge some more. "Wow!" I gasped. My eyes weren't fooling me.

The round sponge moved in my hand, gently and slowly, in and out, in and out in a lazy rhythm.

As if it were breathing!

But sponges don't breathe. Do they?

This one sure did!

I could even hear its little breaths: *Whoa-ahhh, whoa-ahhh*.

"Daniel! I don't think this is just a sponge," I stammered. "I think it's alive!" I tossed it back into the sink cabinet. I admit it. I felt a little scared.

My brother put his hands on his hips. "That's a pretty lame joke," he snickered.

"But, Daniel —" I started.

"You can't get me with that one, Kat. It's an old sponge," he insisted, grinning. "A dirty old sponge that's probably been here for a hundred years."

"All right, don't believe me!" I exclaimed. "When I'm famous for discovering this thing, I won't tell them you're my brother."

Mom walked by, carrying an armload of winter coats. I knew that she would believe me.

"Mom!" I yelled. "The sponge! It's alive!"

"That's nice, dear," she murmured. "Only a few more things to bring in. Now, where did I put that box of silverware?"

My mother acted as if she didn't even hear me! "Mom," I started again, even louder this time. "The sponge! Under the sink! It's breathing!"

She ignored me and kept walking through the kitchen and right out the screen door into the backyard.

Nobody cared about my amazing find.

Except for Killer. He seemed really interested.

Maybe too interested.

Killer bent his neck down low, poked his head into the cabinet, gave the sponge a long stare — and growled, deep in his throat.

Grrrr. Grrrr.

Why was he growling again?

Killer touched his wet nose to the sponge. He shoved it around, sniffing and sniffing. He gazed up at me for a moment, a puzzled expression on his dog face.

Grrrr. Grrrr.

Killer opened his mouth and grabbed the sponge in his teeth.

"Hey, that's not lunch!" I yelped, grabbing Killer by his collar and yanking him out from under the sink. "That could be a very important discovery."

I turned to my brother.

"See, Daniel? Killer knows it's alive," I insisted. "Honest, it's not a trick. Look closer — I promise that you'll see it breathing."

Daniel smirked as if he didn't believe me. But he poked his head into the cabinet.

"Hey, whoa! You might be right," he admitted. He pulled himself up to face me. "I think it is alive! And I also think . . . it's *mine!*"

With that, he dove under the sink to grab the sponge.

"No way!" I protested. I grabbed the back of his T-shirt and hauled him out. "I saw it first. The sponge belongs to me!"

He shook me off and dove back down again. "Finders, keepers!" he cried.

I made another grab for him.

But before I could touch him, Daniel uttered a bloodcurdling scream of pain!

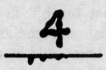

4

"AAAAAIIIIIII!"

You could probably hear Daniel's wail for blocks.

That got Mom's attention. She came banging through the screen door from the backyard.

"What happened? Who screamed? What's wrong? What's going on?" Mom demanded.

Daniel backed out from under the sink, holding his head. He squinted up at us. "I hit my head on the sink," he wailed. "Kat pushed me!"

Mom knelt down and put her arm around Daniel. "You poor thing," she said soothingly. She patted his head softly.

"I did not push him," I declared. "I didn't even touch him."

Daniel groaned and rubbed the side of his head. "It really hurts," he complained. "I'll probably have a huge bump there."

He glared at me. "You did it on purpose! And

14

it's not your sponge, anyway. It was in the house. So it belongs to all of us!"

"It is so my sponge!" I insisted. "What's your problem, Daniel? Why do you always want what's mine?"

"That's enough!" Mom cried impatiently. "I can't believe you're fighting over a stupid sponge!"

Mom turned to me. "Kat, you are supposed to be keeping an eye on your brother, aren't you?" she demanded. "And, Daniel, don't take things that aren't yours."

She turned to leave the room. "Not one more word about a silly sponge! Or you'll both be sorry!"

As soon as Mom left the room, Daniel stuck out his tongue at me and crossed his eyes. "Thanks for getting me in trouble," he grumbled.

He stomped off, with Killer at his heels.

Alone in the kitchen, I bent down, reached my hand under the sink, and picked up the sponge.

"Everyone's yelling and screaming around here," I whispered to it. "You're causing a lot of trouble — aren't you?"

I felt sort of dumb talking to a sponge.

But it didn't feel like a sponge. Not at all.

It's warm, I thought in surprise. Warm and damp.

"Are you alive?" I asked the wrinkled little ball.

I closed my hand around it softly — and the weirdest thing happened. The sponge started moving in my hand.

Well, not exactly moving.

Pulsing — slowly and gently.

Ca-chunk. Ca-chunk.

It moved like the plastic model heart we used in science class.

Could I be feeling a heartbeat?

I peered curiously at the thing. I ran my fingertips over the wrinkles that covered it, pushing back the folds of spongy, moist material.

"Whoa!" I cried, startled. Two wet, black eyes stared out at me.

I shuddered. "Yuck!"

You aren't a sponge at all, I thought. Sponges don't have eyes, do they? What *are* you?

I needed some answers. Quick. But who could I talk to?

Not Mom. She didn't want to hear about the sponge.

"Dad! Dad!" I called out, dashing through the living room and dining room. "Where are you?"

"Mmmmph," he shouted. "Mmmmmpph."

"What?" I yelled, running through the house. "Oh, here you are."

Dad stood at the top of a ladder in the front hall. He had a hammer in one hand and a big roll of black electrician's tape in the other.

And a bunch of nails in his mouth. "Mmmmpph," he mumbled.

"Dad, what are you trying to say?" I asked.

He spit the nails out.

"Sorry," Dad grumbled. "I've got to get this hall light working. These darn old wires."

He stared down at a pile of tools on the floor. "Kat, hand me those pliers. If this doesn't do it, I'll have to call an electrician."

Dad is great at getting flowers to bloom and grass to grow. But when it comes to handyman stuff, he messes up. A lot.

One time, he tried to fix a fan — and knocked out the electricity all over the neighborhood.

"Here, Dad." I handed him the pliers and held up the sponge.

"Check this out," I urged. I stood on tiptoes so he could see the sponge up close. "I found it under the sink, and it's warm and it has eyes and it's alive. I can't figure out what it is."

Dad peered out from under his baseball cap. "Let's have a look at that," he offered.

I shoved the sponge up so he could reach it.

He leaned down to grab the sponge from me.

I didn't see the ladder wobble.

And I didn't see it start to tilt over.

I only saw Dad's expression change. I saw his eyes go wide. And his mouth open in a startled scream.

As he started to fall, he grabbed at the light in the ceiling for support.

"Nooooooo!"

The light came crashing down on his head.
Dad sailed off the top of the ladder.
He lay on the hall floor, perfectly still.
"Mom! Mo-om! Mom!" I shrieked. "Come quick! It's Dad!"

5

Mom, Daniel, and I huddled around Dad. His eyes fluttered open. He blinked.

"Huh?" he murmured. "What happened?"

Dad shook his head and pushed himself up onto his elbows. "I think I'm okay, guys," he said shakily.

Dad tried to stand up. But he collapsed to the floor. "My ankle. I think it may be broken." He groaned in pain.

With me on one side and Mom on the other, we helped Dad to the couch. "Oof, that really hurts," he moaned. He rubbed the ankle tenderly.

"Daniel, go put some ice into a towel for your father," Mom instructed. "Kat, get him a cold drink."

"Now, honey," Mom whispered, wiping Dad's brow, "tell me what happened."

When I came running back into the living room with a tall glass of ice water, Mom and Dad had the weirdest expressions on their faces.

"Kat," said Mom angrily, "did you push your father?"

"Why did you push the ladder?" Dad asked, rubbing his ankle.

"Huh? Excuse me?" I spluttered. "I didn't push you! I wouldn't!"

"We'll discuss this later, young lady," Mom said sternly. "For now, I've got to take care of your father."

She leaned over and applied the ice pack to Dad's swelling ankle.

I felt a hot red flush of embarrassment creep over my face. How could Dad think I pushed him?

I lowered my eyes and realized I still held the sponge.

And I realized something else. Something strange and scary.

Instead of pulsing gently, the sponge *throbbed* in my hand. Throbbed wildly.

Ba-boom, ba-boom, ba-boom.

Vibrating — as if someone had turned a blender to high speed. The sponge practically purred with excitement.

Whoa-ahhh. Whoa-ahhh.

I sat down on the hall floor, feeling shaky.

What's going on here? I wondered. Daniel thought I pushed him. And then Dad said the same thing.

They both think I pushed them. Why?

20

Ba-boom. Ba-boom. Ba-boom. The sponge throbbed warmly in my hand.

I shivered with fear. Suddenly, the sponge seemed kind of scary. I didn't want the thing anywhere near me — or my family.

I ran outside. I found a big metal garbage can near the garage. I lifted the lid. Dropped the sponge inside. Pushed the lid shut firmly.

Back inside the house, Mom called me into the living room. "I think Dad's ankle is only sprained," she said. "Now, tell me what happened."

Thursday, I sat at my desk, writing down the names of guests for my birthday party. The big day was only two days away.

I had to give the list to Mom today, so she could buy enough favors by Saturday.

I heard Daniel babbling away to Carlo as the two boys clambered noisily up the stairs.

"Check it out — it looks like an old sponge. But it's alive!" Daniel explained. "I bet it's a prehistoric creature, like a dinosaur or something."

I jumped up and ran out of my room.

"Hey!" I yelled at Daniel. "What are you doing with that?" I pointed at the sponge in his hands. "I threw that thing away."

"I found it in the garbage can," Daniel replied. "It's too cool to throw away. Right, Carlo?"

Carlo shrugged, his shaggy black hair touching

his shoulders. "It looks like an old sponge. What's the big deal?"

"It's a very big deal," I shot back. "And that thing is definitely not a sponge."

I pulled a large book from my new bookcase. "I checked the encyclopedia," I explained. "Under sponges. You should have left it in the trash, Daniel. You really should have."

"What did the encyclopedia say?" Daniel asked eagerly, plopping down on my bed. He held the sponge between his hands.

"It said that sponges do not have eyes," I replied. "And they can live only in the water. If they're out of the water for more than thirty minutes, they die."

"See, Carlo? It's not a sponge," Daniel declared. "Our creature has eyes. It's been out of water since we found it."

"Well, I don't see any eyes. And it sure doesn't look alive to me," said Carlo doubtfully.

Daniel leaped off the bed and offered his friend the sponge. "Hold it. You'll see."

Carlo carefully cradled the sponge in his hands. His big brown eyes grew wide. "It's warm! And . . . and . . . it's moving. It's squirming! It *is* alive."

Carlo spun around to face me. "But if it's not a sponge, then . . . then, what is it?"

"I haven't figured that out yet," I admitted.

"Maybe it's some kind of a super-sponge," Daniel offered. "So powerful that it can live on land."

"It could be part sponge and part another animal," added Carlo, gazing at it. "Can I take it home for a while? It'll really spook Sandy."

Sandy is Carlo's baby-sitter. "I'll bring it right back," Carlo promised.

"No way, Carlo," I said quickly. "I think I'll keep the sponge right here until I know exactly what it is. Here — stick it in this old gerbil cage."

"Aw, come on," Carlo begged, petting the sponge on the top of its wrinkled head. "See? It likes me."

"No way!" I replied. "Daniel, tell your friend to quit bugging me."

"Okay, okay," Carlo muttered. "Hey, what does this little guy eat, anyway?"

"I don't know," I replied. "But it seems to be fine without eating. Put it in the cage."

Carlo reached into the gerbil cage and set the creature down. As he did, his face filled with horror.

I saw his arm tremble.

Then he let out a terrified scream.

"Aaagh! My hand! It ate my hand!"

6

"Noooo!" I shrieked.

His mouth twisted in horror, Carlo yanked his arm from the gerbil cage — and shoved it in my face.

"Oh!" I gasped.

Carlo wiggled his hand in my face and began to laugh. His hand was perfectly okay.

"You are horrible!" I yelled. "That is so completely *not* funny. It's sick!"

Carlo and Daniel collapsed with laughter.

"Excellent joke!" Daniel grinned. "Hey, Carlo. Give me a . . . hand! Haw, haw, haw."

He and Carlo slapped each other high fives. "Way to go, dude!" Daniel cried.

I glared at the dumb, immature brats.

"You know, guys, this isn't funny," I said seriously. "We don't know what kind of creature the sponge is."

"We don't know what kind of creature you are, either!" Daniel announced with a big grin.

24

"If I'm a creature, you're a creature's baby brother!" I shot back.

"Hey, I have an idea," said Carlo, winking at Daniel. "Maybe you should put the sponge on a leash and take it for a walk. The exercise will give it an appetite!" He hooted with laughter.

He really cracked himself up.

"But it doesn't have legs," Daniel chimed in.

"She can roll it down Maple Lane!" Carlo suggested.

More laughter.

"That's it, you guys. Get out!" I shouted. "Leave me and the sponge alone! Now!"

Slapping each other another high five, Daniel and Carlo turned to leave.

I could hardly wait for them to go. I needed to be by myself for a while. To sit and figure out what I should do with the little round creature.

But before Carlo and Daniel got out the bedroom door, a scream made me nearly jump to the ceiling.

I turned to see Carlo hopping frantically up and down on one foot.

"Oh, right," I said. "Like I'm going to believe another one of your stupid jokes."

Carlo, his face twisted in pain, pointed wildly to his foot. Falling back onto the bed with a groan, he yanked off his sneaker.

Blood oozed through his white sock.

"A nail!" he gasped. "I stepped on a nail!"

I dropped my eyes to the sneaker on the floor.

A long nail had poked through the thick rubber sole — and into Carlo's foot!

Weird, I thought. Where did a nail come from?

"Hey, it's really bleeding!" Carlo wailed. "Do something!"

I searched around frantically for something to use as a bandage. As I did, my eyes rested on the sponge in the gerbil cage.

"Whoa!" I cried.

The sponge quivered and shook.

It shook with what seemed like *joy*!

And it breathed — so loudly that I could hear the eerie sound from the other side of the room!

Whoa-ahhh. Whoa-ahhh.

As I wrapped an old T-shirt around Carlo's foot, two questions ran through my mind — what in the world is happening here? Why did the sponge creature suddenly get so excited?

I wouldn't find out the frightening truth about the sponge creature until the next day.

When I learned it, I understood why there were so many accidents in our new house.

And it made me wish that I had never opened that cabinet, never reached under the sink, and never found the spongy . . . *thing*.

Because now it was too late.

Too late for us all.

7

"Kat, it's all set." Mom grinned at me the next morning when I walked into the kitchen for breakfast.

"What's all set?" I asked sleepily.

"Your birthday party tomorrow!" Mom replied, giving me a quick hug. Mom's *very* big on hugging.

"How could you forget?" she asked in surprise. "We've been planning your birthday for weeks!"

"My party!" I breathed with delight. "Oh, I can't wait!" I sat down at the table for cornflakes and orange juice.

Birthday parties are a really big deal around the Merton house. Mom always orders a big cake. And she makes all the invitations and decorations by hand.

This year, I helped with the invitations. We cut them out of purple construction paper and used a pink sparkle pen to write the words.

I usually have a theme for my parties. Last year's theme was "Make your own pizza." And it was awesome! My friends talked about it for weeks.

Now that I'm going to be twelve, I decided I'm too old for a theme. So Mom and Dad are taking me and five of my best friends to WonderPark — for the entire day.

WonderPark is definitely the coolest. It has two wave pools, a whole bunch of water slides, and the Monster Masher. That's the scariest upside-down roller coaster I've ever been on!

Just how cool is it? Well, last summer, Carlo lost his lunch after a ride on the Masher.

Pretty cool.

"This is going to be my best birthday ever!" I exclaimed, smiling across the table at Mom. I turned to Daniel. "Sorry, you're not invited. This is for twelve-year-olds only."

"No fair! Why *can't* I come along?" he complained, banging his spoon into his cereal and splashing milk all over the table. "I promise I won't talk to any of Kat's friends. Who would *want* to? Please let me come!"

I started to feel sort of bad. I started to change my mind.

And then Daniel totally ruined his chance.

He folded his arms over his chest. "Kat gets everything around here," he grumbled. "She won't even share the sponge with me!"

"That old thing Kat found under the sink?" Mom asked in surprise. "Who'd want it?"

"Me!" yelled Daniel.

"Well, I found it, so it's mine. And I'm bringing *my* sponge to school today," I informed Daniel.

"Why?" Mom asked.

"I'm going to show it to Mrs. Vanderhoff," I explained. "Maybe she'll know what it is. Now I need to find a carrier for *my* sponge."

I searched around in the kitchen cabinets. "Perfect!" I proclaimed, holding up a plastic container labeled DELI. It still smelled faintly of potato salad.

With an old pair of scissors, I punched a few air holes in the top of the container. Then I ran upstairs to get the sponge.

Back in the kitchen, I set the sealed container on the floor and opened the refrigerator.

"Mom," I called, "which lunch bag is mine?"

"The blue one, honey," she replied.

I grabbed my lunch and shut the refrigerator.

I heard a sniffing sound coming from the kitchen floor. I looked down.

"Killer, what are you doing, boy?" I smiled at the floppy-eared dog.

Snrff. Snrff. Snrff.

He sniffed at the container.

Grrr. Grrr.

He pawed the ground and growled.

Here we go again, I thought.

Killer set his ears back, circling the container suspiciously.

And barked.

And barked. And barked.

"Killer! Get back!" I shouted.

But the dog was way too excited to listen to me.

"Mom, Daniel!" I called. "Help me get Killer away. I think he wants to eat the sponge for breakfast!"

Mom grabbed Killer by his collar and hauled him, still growling, away from the container. She pushed the door open and shooed the dog into the backyard. "Go outside, boy, there you go," she said gently.

Mom turned to me. "What's got that dog so upset? He sure is acting strange. Now get a move on, or you'll be late for school. And then *I'll* be growling and barking!"

Throwing my backpack over my shoulder, I gave Mom a quick kiss good-bye and followed Daniel out the door.

"Watch this!" he yelled, dashing across the street to the Johnsons' house and planting himself underneath their basketball hoop.

Daniel faked a dribble and a pass, and ran madly around in circles. "Bet you can't jump this high!" he said, pretending to sink a basket.

"Come on, Daniel," I replied, walking quickly down the street. "Mrs. Vanderhoff will keep me after school if I show up late."

Daniel trotted over to me. Suddenly, his eyes bulged!

"Kat! Look out!" he screamed.

Craaack!

I heard a frightening sound above my head. A loud cracking. As if someone had cracked about a thousand knuckles at the same time.

I glanced up in time to see a huge dead tree branch hurtling down through the air.

I froze.

I couldn't scream. I couldn't move.

I couldn't move a muscle.

I was about to be crushed into Kat litter!

"Ohhhhhhh." A terrified moan escaped my throat.

I felt someone shove me hard from behind.

The force of it sent me flying to the ground.

I lay there in shock and watched the huge tree branch crash down to the ground, cracking and shattering.

It landed a few feet behind me.

As I struggled to pull myself up, the sponge container rolled out of my hand. The little creature came spilling out onto the sidewalk.

"Saved your life!" cried Daniel. "Now you owe me big!"

I barely heard him.

The sponge. I could only stare at the sponge.

Whoa-ahhh, whoa-ahhh.

Breathing louder and faster and deeper than I'd ever heard before.

Whoa-ahhh, whoa-ahhh.

Throbbing its little heart out. Practically hopping around on the ground in excitement.

Ba-boom, ba-boom.

Very weird. I'd almost been killed by the falling branch. And the sponge seemed really excited.

As if it enjoyed my near accident.

As if my accident made it really happy.

"Mrs. Vanderhoff!" I called, rushing into the classroom. "I have to show you something!"

Mrs. Vanderhoff is a *brain.* She basically knows everything about everything.

She's very smart. *And* she takes us on great class trips. At Halloween, we visited a spooky old theater that's supposed to be haunted by the ghosts of dead actors.

But Mrs. Vanderhoff is also really strict. Anyone who goofs off or talks out of turn stays after school for a week!

One other problem. She has no sense of humor at all. I've never even seen her crack a smile.

"Check this out, Mrs. Vanderhoff," I blurted out, shoving the sponge under her nose. "I found it under the kitchen sink of our new house. And when Daniel went to grab it, he hit his head. And my Dad thought I pushed him, and — and —"

Mrs. Vanderhoff peered at me over her wire-rim glasses. "Kat, sshh," she ordered sharply. "Now, start over — slowly and clearly."

I took a deep breath and began again, starting with moving day and ending with the falling tree branch.

"And you say it throbs and breathes?" Mrs. Vanderhoff asked, staring hard at me.

"Yes!" I exclaimed.

"Let me see it," Mrs. Vanderhoff replied. I handed over the container.

Hesitantly, she stuck her hand in and lifted the sponge out.

"Oh, wow." I groaned in disappointment. The sponge appeared dry and shriveled.

It didn't breathe. It didn't throb.

Mrs. Vanderhoff glared at me. "Kat, what's the meaning of this?" she huffed. "This is an ordinary kitchen sponge."

She made a face. "A dirty one, I might add."

"You're wrong!" I cried shrilly, desperate for her to believe me. "It's much more than a sponge. It's alive. It has eyes — see? You've got to see!"

Mrs. Vanderhoff squinted at me, shaking her gray-haired head.

"Oh, all right," she said with a sigh. She bent her head and examined the sponge closely. She ran her fingers over its wrinkled surface.

"I don't know what in the world you're talking about," she said angrily, motioning for me to take my seat. "This thing doesn't have eyes. And it's not alive. It's a dirty, dried-up old sponge."

Mrs. Vanderhoff glared at me. "If this is your idea of a joke, Katrina, I don't get it. I don't get it at all."

"But . . ." I started.

Mrs. Vanderhoff held up her hand. "Not another word," she instructed. She handed the sponge back — dropping it into my hand like a piece of junk.

My stomach churned with disappointment.

Couldn't I say anything else to convince her?

The sharp rap of a ruler on her desk interrupted my thoughts. "I'm going to pass back the papers from your math test last week," Mrs. Vanderhoff announced.

Everyone groaned. The surprise quiz on long division had been a major disaster for all of us.

"Settle down," Mrs. Vanderhoff snapped.

She reached into her desk to pull out the test papers, and — *slammed her fingers in the drawer!*

With a howl of pain, she shrieked, "My fingers! Owww — I think I broke my fingers!"

I was still standing beside her desk. Holding her hand, she turned to me. "Help me, Katrina. I've got to get to the nurse's office!"

I opened the classroom door for Mrs. Vanderhoff. Then I helped her down the hall to the infirmary.

"What's happened?" Mrs. Twitchell, the school nurse, jumped up from her desk and came running up to us. Her starchy white uniform rustled as she moved. She sat Mrs. Vanderhoff in a comfortable chair.

"My fingers," groaned Mrs. Vanderhoff, holding up her red, swollen hand. "I smashed them in the desk drawer!"

"All right," Mrs. Twitchell said soothingly. "We'll put some ice on that hand. And I'll make sure the principal sends somebody to watch your class."

"Thank you," Mrs. Vanderhoff moaned. "Katrina, you can go on back to class now. You've been very helpful."

Helpful?

Everywhere I went these days, I told myself, somebody seemed to get badly hurt!

Unhappily, I shuffled my way back toward classroom 6B.

"Kat! Kat!" I heard someone shouting my name.

Daniel raced out of the library, nearly tripping over his untied shoelaces. He crashed right into me.

"I found it!" he cried breathlessly. "I found the sponge creature! In a book! I know what it is!"

9

I grabbed Daniel by the front of his shirt. "What is it? What?" I demanded. "I have to know!"

"Whoa. Take it easy. Cool your jets." Daniel pushed my hands off his shirt. "I'll *show* you," he promised. "I have a picture in here."

"In where?" I asked.

Daniel gazed around the hall. No one in sight.

He pulled a book out from under his shirt and handed it to me. A big black volume.

I glanced quickly at the title: *Encyclopedia of the Weird*.

"Is your picture in there?" I teased.

"Ha-ha. Very funny," he replied. He grabbed the book away from me. "Do you want to see your sponge?"

"Definitely!"

Daniel flipped the pages quickly, muttering to himself, "Grebles, Griffins, Grocks. Here it is!"

He shoved the book under my nose. It smelled

funny — sort of musty. I guessed it had been sitting on the library shelf a long, long time.

Daniel pointed to a drawing on page 89. I lowered my eyes to the page.

Wrinkly skin. Tiny black eyes. "It *does* look like the sponge," I gasped.

I began reading the story underneath the drawing.

"This is a Grool."

A Grool? I thought. What in the world is that? I returned to the book:

"The Grool is an ancient and mythical creature."

"Mythical?" I cried. "That means it's not real — that it's made up! But it *is* real!"

"Keep reading," Daniel urged.

"The Grool does not eat food or drink water. Instead, it gets its strength from luck. Bad luck."

"Daniel," I stammered. "This is weird. Really weird." He nodded, his eyes wide.

"The Grool has always been known as a bad-luck charm. It feeds on the bad luck of other people. The Grool becomes stronger each time something bad happens around it."

"This book is crazy," I muttered. I eagerly read some more: *"Bad luck for the Grool owner never ends. The Grool cannot be killed — by force or by any violent means. And it cannot — ever — be given away or tossed aside."*

Why not? I wondered.

The next lines gave me the answer:

"A Grool is only passed on to a new owner when an owner dies. Anyone who gives the Grool away will DIE within one day."

"That is so stupid!" I exclaimed. "Stupid. Stupid. Stupid."

Turning to Daniel, I said in a low voice, "There is no such thing as a creature that lives on bad luck."

"How do *you* know, genius?" Daniel demanded.

"Everything needs food and water," I replied. "Everything that's alive, anyway."

"I don't know," Daniel said. "I think the book could be right."

The drawing of a creature on another page caught my eye. "Hey, what's this?" I asked.

It looked like a potato — oval and brown. But it had a mouth full of sharp, pointy teeth.

I quickly read the description.

"The Lanx is a cousin of the Grool. But it is much more dangerous."

"Yuck!" Daniel cried, making a face.

I kept reading:

"Once the Lanx latches on to someone, it never lets go — until it has drained every drop of energy from that person."

I slammed the encyclopedia shut. "Here, Daniel, take this dumb book!" I shoved the *Encyclo-*

pedia of the Weird back into my brother's arms. "This stuff is totally crazy. I don't believe any of it."

"But I thought you wanted to know more about the sponge," Daniel said.

"I do. But not this made-up stuff!" I told him.

I knew I was acting sort of rotten to Daniel. And that he only wanted to help.

But give me a break. After all that had been happening, I was a little stressed out.

I mean, it had been a bad couple of days — with Dad falling off the ladder, and Mrs. Vanderhoff slamming her hand in the desk.

And me nearly being crushed by the tree branch!

I stomped down the hall back to class. "Stupid book," I muttered to myself.

But another thought kept forcing its way into my mind: *What if the book is right?*

I stared at the Grool, still sitting in its container on the corner of Mrs. Vanderhoff's desk. I walked up to it.

It was wet again. And breathing. Its cold, black eyes stared back.

I felt a chill of fear and a prickling all over my skin.

"Mythical creatures don't exist," I whispered to the creature. "I'm not going to believe that book. I'm not!"

The sponge stared up at me, breathing softly.

I picked up the container and shook it angrily. "What are you?" I cried. "What?"

Daniel told Carlo the whole story on the walk home. I walked behind them, trying to think about something else. *Anything* else.

"It's called a Grool. And it's a bad-luck charm," Daniel explained excitedly. "Right, Kat?"

"I think *you're* the bad-luck charm," I snapped. "And I don't think that book makes any sense."

"Oh, yeah?" he cried. He grabbed my backpack.

"You don't need these books, do you?" he teased. "You're so smart, you know more than the encyclopedia."

Dancing down the street with my books, Daniel turned on to Maple Lane. "Hey, Mom's outside!" he cried, surprised. He started to run.

Carlo and I hurried to catch up with Daniel.

Mom stood at the door, waiting for us. Her face wore a tense, worried expression. "Hi, kids. Come on inside," she said.

Daniel, Carlo, and I followed Mom into the kitchen.

"I'm afraid I have some very bad news," she began sadly.

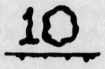

10

"Killer is gone," Mom announced. She bit her lower lip.

"Gone?" Daniel and I shrieked at once.

"He ran away," Mom explained. "I can't find him anywhere. He must have slipped out when I went to put some things in the garage."

"But, Mom —" I protested. "Killer never runs away. He's never done it before."

"Kat is right!" Daniel agreed. "He's not brave enough to run away."

"Don't worry," Mom said. "I'm sure we'll find him. I've called the police, and they're out searching for him right now."

"*I'll* find Killer," Daniel cried. "Bet I can find him before the police! Come on, Carlo!"

Daniel grabbed a handful of doggie treats and ran out. Carlo followed close behind.

The door slammed shut behind them.

Poor Killer, I thought. Out somewhere alone. Probably lost. Bet he's scared.

Our new house is so close to the highway — to all those speeding cars. What will happen to my little dog?

I suddenly felt like crying. I grabbed the sponge in its container and ran up the stairs.

"It's all your fault, isn't it?" I accused the creature. "I bet you *are* a Grool after all!"

As I talked, the Grool pulsed. It shook so hard, I expected it to throb right out of the container.

Ba-boom. Ba-boom.

And it breathed fast and deep.

Whoa-ahhh. Whoa-ahhh.

I yanked the Grool out. "We've had enough bad luck!" I wailed. "Maybe *this* will stop you!" I hurled the horrible thing as hard as I could against the wall.

The Grool hit the wall with a sickening *splat*.

And I let out a shrill cry of pain.

11

I glanced down and saw red.

Red blood.

Flowing over my left hand.

As I threw the Grool, I slammed the hand down on my desk — onto the sharp point of a pair of scissors!

"Ohhh!" I moaned, checking out my hand. A deep, nasty cut.

I wrapped some tissues around the cut to slow the bleeding. Then I spotted the Grool down on the floor.

Dead, I hoped.

I bent down.

"Gross!" I yelped. The Grool was breathing and throbbing — faster and harder than ever before.

Whoa-ahhh. Whoa-ahhh.

I leaned in closer.

Heh, heh, heh.

"Hey, what's that?" I murmured.

Heh, heh, heh.

I guess you'd call the noise a laugh. A dry, cruel snicker that sounded more like a cough.

Then, as I listened to that evil laugh, the Grool began changing.

Its color suddenly brightened — from dull brown to light pink. As I stared in amazement, the Grool turned bright tomato-red.

As red as the blood on my cut hand.

My hand! Yuck! Blood seeped through the tissues and dripped slowly onto the floor.

I needed help with this. Mom's help.

"Mom!" I called, leaping up. "I need a Band-Aid. A big one!"

As I hurried down the hall, a jumble of questions ran through my mind.

Why did the Grool change color? I wondered. And that laugh — I'd never heard it before. What did it mean? Was it really laughing?

Did I hurt the Grool when I threw it against my bedroom wall? Is that why it turned red?

So many frightening questions. . . .

I listened at the door, cupping my hand around my ear.

Voices. Inside my room.

"Who's there?" I called out shakily.

The door flew open.

"It's the ghost of the Grool," Daniel whispered in a spooky voice. "Owoooooooo."

Daniel and Carlo stood over the gerbil cage, giggling.

"Oh, I'm *so* scared," I sneered. "Did you find Killer?"

"No," Daniel replied sadly. "Carlo and I searched all over the neighborhood. Mom says the police will find him."

I turned my eyes to the gerbil cage. "How did the Grool get back in there?"

"I found it on the floor, so I stuck it back in the cage," Daniel replied. "How did it get out?"

"Beats me." I shrugged. I didn't feel like explaining.

Carlo, who'd been studying the Grool closely, stared at me. "Hey, what happened to your hand?" he asked, pointing to my bandage.

I didn't want to tell them.

"Oh, uh, nothing," I replied. "Just a little cut. Why are you guys standing there staring at the Grool?"

"Carlo still wants to borrow it," Daniel explained, tapping the side of the cage to get the creature's attention. "I told him no."

Carlo turned to me. "Please," he begged. "I promise I'll be careful. Please, please, please, please . . ."

That stupid Grool! "Oh, take it and keep it!" I snapped.

"Excellent!" Carlo's eyes lit up, and he reached eagerly into the plastic cage to grab his prize.

"Wait!" Daniel cried, grabbing Carlo's arm to stop him. "Kat, remember what the *Encyclopedia of the Weird* said."

Daniel began reciting the Grool entry from memory, staring at me all the while.

"You cannot give a Grool away. Anyone who gives the Grool away will DIE within one day."

A feeling of dread grew in my stomach.

But I couldn't believe that stupid book. Could I?

Did the encyclopedia say that Grools laugh? Or change color?

No.

Carlo and Daniel stared at me. Waiting for my decision. Should I give the sponge creature to Carlo?

I studied the Grool.

"Don't do it, Kat," Daniel urged. "Please don't give it away. It's too dangerous."

I knew only one thing. I wanted to get the Grool away from me as quickly as I could. And if Carlo wanted it so badly, I decided, let him have it!

"Go ahead, Carlo," I said. "Take the gross, disgusting thing."

Daniel grabbed the Grool out of the cage and held it tightly. "No!" he cried. "Carlo is *not* taking it. I don't care what you say. I won't let him take it!"

"Now who's the scaredy-cat?" I asked, giving Daniel a poke in the arm.

"I'm trying to save *you*!" Daniel exclaimed. "Don't you understand?"

Poor Daniel. He seemed so serious, so frightened. I decided to give him a break.

"Well, okay. Carlo, I guess you'd better not take the Grool," I announced.

Daniel heaved a sigh of relief.

Carlo frowned. "Okay. Bye. I'm out of here."

"I'll go with you," Daniel said, tossing the Grool back into the cage. "Come on, let's ride our bikes to the park. Maybe Killer's there." As he hurried out of the bedroom, Daniel turned and gave me a thumbs-up.

After the boys left, I collapsed on my bed. What's going to happen next? I wondered.

I lifted my eyes to the plastic cage and glared at the Grool. I felt a deep hatred for the little creature.

"If one more bad thing happens around here, I'll bury you," I promised it. "I'll bury you so far in the ground that no one will ever find you or see you again. Ever."

It was a promise I would soon have to keep.

12

The next morning I woke up with a jolt.

Toot! Toot! Daniel stood at the foot of my bed, blowing away on a party horn.

"Time to get up, Kat!" he squealed.

I reached out to grab the noisy horn away. "Quit it, you loser!" I grumbled. Then I remembered.

My birthday! Finally! Something to celebrate.

I jumped out of bed. Time to get ready to go to WonderPark!

I planned to be on the Seattle Log Flume and the Wild Wave Slide all day long!

Running to the window, I peeked out through the glass. "No!" I cried in disappointment. "No! It can't be!"

Rain poured down. Lightning crackled through the sky. Thunder boomed so loud, I felt the house shake.

How could we go to WonderPark in this mess?

"Kat," Mom called from downstairs. "Breakfast."

I threw on my purple-and-pink-striped leggings and a purple T-shirt and ran to the kitchen. On my birthday Mom always makes my favorite — waffles with strawberries and powdered sugar.

"Here's the birthday girl. Happy birthday, honey." Mom beamed, giving me a big hug.

"I'm dressed for my party," I said hopefully as I sat down at the table.

"Oh, honey, I'm afraid we'll have to cancel your party," Mom said sadly. "We certainly can't go to WonderPark in this storm."

Cancel? I poked unhappily at my waffles.

"Can't we have the party here — indoors?" I pleaded. "We'll order pizza and play computer games in the den."

"You know that we can't do that," Mom said. "The painters will be here all day in the living room and dining room. With all those ladders and buckets of paint, I can't have your friends running around."

What rotten luck.

"But, Mom, it's my birthday!" I protested, throwing down my fork. "And you promised I could have a party. You promised!"

Mom sighed. "I know how disappointed you are, Kat. We'll have your party another day. Maybe next weekend."

Another day wouldn't be my birthday. "Everything's going wrong!" I cried. "Ever since we moved!"

I hated this new house. I even hated my birthday.

Most of all, I hated the Grool.

Leaving my waffles on the plate, I ran up to my room. I snatched the Grool out of its cage and shook it as hard as I could.

"I warned you!" I threatened. "You ruined my birthday! Now you'll pay!"

The Grool throbbed happily in my hand, and I hurled it back into the gerbil cage. "I hate you!" I shrieked. "I really hate you! You and your bad luck!"

Plopping down at my desk, I decided I *had* to take action. Strong action.

No birthday party. No more Grool.

"I'm keeping my promise," I told the creature.

I pulled a notebook out of my desk drawer and began to make some plans to get rid of it.

"Daniel, it's not raining anymore," I whispered to my brother. "Come on, it's time."

The Grool vibrated in its plastic container.

Ba-boom. Ba-boom.

Daniel glanced up from his computer screen. "Now?" he asked. "Give me a break, Kat. I'm on level ten, and I need to slay only one more troll before I can open the treasure chest."

"This is important. *Really* important," I insisted.

51

Daniel sighed. "Do you think you should do it? You know what the book said."

"I've got to!" I cried. "Remember, it's the Grool's fault that Killer ran away."

Daniel was definitely nervous. And scared.

But he obediently hit the *save* button on *Troll Terror* and followed me outside to the backyard. It had rained all day. But now a few stars shone high above us in the charcoal night sky.

"Here. You hold the Grool," I whispered. I shoved the creature into his trembling hands.

I skipped over to the garage — feeling happy for the first time in days. "I'm getting rid of the Grool," I sang to myself.

Grabbing the biggest shovel I could find, I made my way back to Daniel. Then I started to dig.

This had to be a serious hole, a deep hole. Something the Grool could never, ever climb out of.

A cool breeze blew around me. But digging in the damp ground was hard work. Sweat rolled down my back and forehead.

I didn't feel scared at all. I had to do *something* to make life normal again. I had to stop all the bad luck.

And if it meant burying a living sponge, fine. As long as I never had to see that stupid, snickering creature again.

I peered down into the hole. It seemed pretty deep, about as long as my arm.

"I'm finished," I told my brother. "Pass me the Grool."

Daniel silently handed the sponge to me.

As I held it over the deep hole, the sponge didn't throb. It didn't breathe. It didn't even feel warm.

It felt dry and dead, like an ordinary kitchen sponge.

But I knew better.

I dropped the Grool into the hole and watched happily as it tumbled down the steep dirt sides to the bottom.

Picking up the shovel again, I began throwing dirt onto the creature — heap after heap.

Dig. Throw. Dig. Throw.

Finally, the hole was filled up. I used the back of the shovel to smooth the dirt flat. "There," I said. "No one but us will know the Grool is buried here."

I lowered my eyes to the soft, wet dirt. "Bye, bye Grool," I called out happily. "Daniel, I think our luck is going to change now."

Daniel didn't reply.

I spun around. "Daniel? Daniel? Where are you?"

My brother had disappeared.

13

What had I done?

I dropped the shovel in a panic. "Daniel!" I shrieked. "Where are you?"

Had I made my brother disappear? Did burying the Grool somehow make Daniel vanish into thin air?

"Daniel? Daniel?" I called in a trembling voice.

I heard a soft rustling sound coming from behind the garage.

I crept quietly toward it. "Daniel," I whispered. "Is that you?"

No reply.

I peeked behind the garage.

Daniel sat with his arms locked around his knees. Safe and sound.

"Daniel!" I cried. I felt so relieved that I pinched him.

"Cut it out," he snapped. He leaped to his feet.

"What are you doing back here? I was so worried — I thought the Grool got you!"

Daniel didn't reply. He lowered his eyes to the ground.

"Why did you hide?" I demanded.

"I was scared," he murmured. "I thought the Grool might explode or fight back or something."

"You were scared?" I asked. "Why didn't you at least answer me when I called you?"

"I thought maybe the Grool was chasing you," he confessed, his face turning red.

"Daniel, don't worry," I said. The poor guy was really frightened. And embarrassed that he had hid.

I put both hands on his shoulders. "The Grool is gone. It's buried deep in the ground."

He swallowed hard. "But what if it comes back? What if what the book said comes true?"

"We'll never see the Grool again," I said quietly. "And don't forget — the book said Grools don't really exist. It's all made up. Just a myth, a fairy tale."

Daniel sighed. "I hate to admit it, but you're right, Kat," he said. "At least this time."

"*This* time?" I shot back. "How about all the time?" I slugged Daniel on the arm.

"Oh, that hurts so much I think I'm going to pass out!" Daniel cried sarcastically. He fell on to the wet lawn and pretended to faint.

"Come on, let's go in," I urged. "You're getting soaked. And I'm covered with dirt."

Daniel scrambled up and elbowed me aside.

"Race you!" he cried, running toward the house.

I leaped up the steps and beat him into the house by about a second. I slammed the screen door and held it closed, so Daniel couldn't open it.

"I won!" I shouted.

"Only because I let you," Daniel cried. He banged on the door.

"Do you want to get in here?" I asked.

Daniel nodded.

"Then say, 'Kat beat me fair and square,' " I commanded.

"No way!" he replied.

"Stay out there all night, then — with the Groooooooool!" I told him. I let out a ghostly howl.

"Okay, okay. Kat beat me fair and square," Daniel grumbled. "But I'll win next time!"

Actually, I didn't really care about the race. I felt so glad that I buried the Grool, I would have let Daniel win *ten* races.

As we burst into the living room, Mom and Dad raised their eyes from their newspapers. The house smelled of fresh paint.

"Where were you?" Dad asked.

"Oh, just fooling around in the yard," I replied.

"Is everything all right?" Mom asked with concern. "You're filthy!"

"Everything is fine," I answered. "Now."

"Okay, go and wash up," Mom ordered. "Then come into the kitchen."

Daniel and I crowded into the bathroom, leaned

over the sink, pushing and bumping each other, and cleaned ourselves up.

"Do you know what time it is?" Mom asked as I raced back into the kitchen.

"Yes!" I shouted happily. "It's time for my birthday cake."

Mom beamed. "Well, sit right down here."

I dropped excitedly into the chair she offered. Finally, I thought, things are going right again.

Daniel perched on the chair next to mine. He grabbed my arm. "Something bad is going to happen," he whispered. "I know it. I just know it."

I'm not going to let anything wreck tonight, I thought.

"Don't be such a wimp," I whispered. "Everything's fine."

At the kitchen counter, Mom hovered over the cake. She touched a match to each of the thirteen candles — one for each year and an extra one for luck.

What an awesome cake! Mom had ordered it from the bakery down the street. It had all my favorites: pink frosting roses, chocolate icing, and a layer of strawberries. A tiny chocolate Ferris wheel sat on top.

"Ready, Kat?" Mom asked. She carried the cake to the table. Her faced glowed happily in the candlelight. Dad flashed me a big grin.

They all began to sing "Happy Birthday."

I saw Daniel watching me closely as he sang.

They finished the song. I shut my eyes and made my wishes.

"I wish Killer would come home," I said to myself. "And I wish the Grool would never return. And that Daniel is wrong — that nothing bad will happen."

I leaned forward, closer to the candles, and blew hard.

Pop!

The loud noise from the kitchen nearly made me fall into my cake!

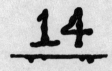

14

"Boy, that cork was loud!" chirped Mom.

She set down a tray of glasses and a large green bottle. "It's your favorite — sparkling apple cider," she announced. "I know it's not as good as a day at WonderPark. . . ."

"Oh, Mom!" I gasped, my heart still pounding. "It's great. Everything is going to be great."

An excellent birthday. Cake, sparkling cider, and presents — two new video games, a Discman and some CDs, a purple backpack, and a sweat-shirt in pink and purple — my favorite colors.

That night before bed, I stuffed my school books into my new backpack. I stared at the gerbil cage. Empty and clean — as if the Grool had never even existed.

I got rid of the disgusting creature, I thought happily. I really did.

My family will finally be safe from bad luck.

The clock in the hall room chimed ten. Time for

bed. I climbed into my nightshirt and dove under the covers.

When the alarm rang the next morning, I bounced out of bed and ran to the window to check the weather.

"Oh, nooo!"

I uttered a low moan of horror.

The backyard — it looked like a desert!

Overnight, the grass had all burned brown. All the pink begonias dropped to the ground, dead and brown. Dad's red roses had shriveled and turned black.

Poor Dad, I thought. He worked so hard to make the yard beautiful. And, now . . .

As I stared at the ugly, dead yard, I tried to force the thought from my mind. But deep down inside, I knew *exactly* how it all happened.

The Grool.

From its grave, the Grool had turned its evil powers on the lawn. And it killed every single living plant, flower, and blade of grass!

What should I do? I wondered, staring out at the burned, dried-out, dead, dead yard.

Should I remove the Grool from the ground?

Did I have a choice?

Not really.

I quickly pulled on my new sweatshirt and a pair of jeans. Then I crept downstairs. I sneaked out to the spot where I had buried the Grool.

And I began to dig.

Brown, dry leaves rained down on my head. My shoulder ached from lifting the damp, heavy dirt. My stomach didn't feel too great, either.

Dig, toss. Dig, toss.

The more I dug, the worse I felt.

I wanted to throw the shovel down and run from the spot. To leave the terrible creature buried for good.

But I had to face the truth.

If I left the Grool buried, it would keep on punishing me. It would punish my whole family.

I dug to the bottom of the hole. Then I bent down and pushed the dirt away with both hands.

Slowly, before my frightened eyes, the Grool throbbed into view. More alive and excited than ever.

"I should smash you with this shovel!" I yelled at it.

The Grool vibrated crazily, almost as if what I said made it happy.

Ba-boom. Ba-boom. I could hear it breathe.

And then once again, it turned from brown to pink to tomato-red. And it *kept* changing color as it breathed.

Brown. Pink. Red.

Brown. Pink. Red.

I grabbed the Grool from its grave. It pulsed so hard that it throbbed right out of my hand and fell to the ground.

"Stay still!" I shrieked, snatching it up.

The Grool stared at me. Its tiny, round eyes glowed red with evil.

I shivered.

I gritted my teeth and shoved the Grool into the pocket of my new sweatshirt. I trudged back to the house, through the kitchen door, and into the hall that led to the stairs.

At the bottom of the stairs, I heard a noise. It came from Mom and Dad's bedroom.

They're awake, I thought. I've got to hurry before they see me and ask questions. That's all I need.

I leaped up the stairs, taking them two at a time.

Whomp! I slipped and landed hard on my right knee. "Ouch!" I shrieked.

I felt the Grool shake in my pocket. I heard its ugly, soft snicker.

Heh, heh, heh.

It was laughing at me!

I jerked it out of my pocket and squeezed it so hard that my fingers hurt. Then I ran to my room and threw the Grool into the gerbil cage.

"I'll find a way to destroy you," I promised. I rubbed my aching knee and glared at the little beast. "Before you can bring us any more bad luck, I will destroy you!" I cried.

But how? I wondered.

How?

15

"Kids, Aunt Louise is coming tomorrow," Mom told Daniel and me the next morning. "So I want you both to clean up your rooms after school today."

"Aunt Louise is coming?" I asked. "Great!"

Aunt Louise is my favorite aunt. Even though she's a grown-up, she's completely cool.

She wears long, flowery dresses and drives a bright yellow convertible.

And Aunt Louise blows the biggest bubble gum bubbles! And she knows a lot of really funny jokes.

Mom says Aunt Louise has her head in the clouds. I guess that means she has a wild imagination. I don't know about that, but she *does* know a lot about things like astrology and tarot cards.

And, maybe — about Grools.

That night, after I cleaned my room and before I went to bed, I said a *special* good night to the Grool.

"My aunt is coming tomorrow and she's going

to help me get rid of you forever," I whispered.

It stared up at me, breathing softly.

After school the next afternoon, Daniel and I turned the corner onto our block. And we saw Aunt Louise's yellow convertible in the driveway. We ran the rest of the way home.

"Hey — what's up?" Aunt Louise called as we burst into the house. A floppy yellow straw hat covered her black curly hair.

Before Daniel could get to her, I threw my arms around Aunt Louise and whispered in her ear, "Come upstairs with me. *Now*. It's super-important."

My aunt pulled off her hat and set it on my head. She admired me in the hat. "*Super*-important?" she asked.

"Yes," I whispered, grabbing her hand and tugging her toward the stairs.

"Have you ever heard of a Grool?" I asked.

"A Grool? Hmmm. I'll have to think about that one for a minute," she replied thoughtfully. "No, I don't think so. What is a Grool?"

"Well," I explained, "Daniel found a picture in an encyclopedia. And the book said it was an ancient, mythical creature. . . ."

"Well, if it's mythical, honey, that means it doesn't exist," Aunt Louise interrupted.

"But it's *not* mythical!" I cried impatiently. "I

64

should know because I have one. And it causes trouble, lots of trouble."

Aunt Louise followed me to my room.

"Have you ever heard of a Lanx?" I asked.

She shook her head.

"That's another creature in that encyclopedia. It looks like a potato, but it has a mouth full of sharp teeth."

"Good heavens. It sounds disgusting!" Aunt Louise exclaimed. "But tell me about this . . . Grool. What does it look like?"

"Here. I'll show you," I said. I pulled her into my room.

I pointed at the gerbil cage. The Grool squatted in the corner.

Aunt Louise walked up to the cage. "So you're a Grool," she said, leaning down. She reached over to pick it up.

"Wait," I cried. "Maybe you shouldn't touch it."

But I was too late.

16

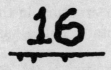

Aunt Louise picked up the Grool and placed it in the palm of her hand. She studied it for a long while.

Then she turned to me. "Kat, it's only a dried-up sponge. What's the big idea?"

"But — but —" I sputtered.

"Oh, I get it!" she laughed. "You really had me fooled! I thought you were serious!" She tossed the Grool to me.

I tried to catch it, but I didn't want to touch it. It plopped to the floor.

"Pretty funny, kid." She chuckled as she turned to leave. "You have a great imagination. Just like your aunt."

I picked up the Grool and examined it closely.

Not warm.

Not breathing.

Not moving at all.

Dry and hard.

An ordinary sponge.

Aunt Louise thought I was joking. But the joke was on me.

The Grool had tricked me again!

I hurled the creature back into the gerbil cage. It lay there lifeless. "I hope you rot in there!" I exploded.

Before my amazed eyes, the dry brown sponge began plumping up. In a few seconds, it became fuller and moister.

"Yuck!" I groaned, watching it turn pink and then red.

The Grool huffed and puffed. *Whoa-ahhhh. Whoa-ahhh.*

Those little black eyes peered out at me excitedly.

The Grool snickered softly.

Why was it so pleased with itself? I wondered. Nothing horrible had happened.

Or had it?

I thought of Dad's fall off the ladder. The tree branch. Mrs. Vanderhoff's fingers. Killer running away. My spoiled birthday party. Our dry, rotted backyard.

It was all too much. Too much!

With a desperate cry, I yanked the evil thing out of its cage. Then I slammed it down hard on my desk.

Breathing hard, my heart pounding, I grabbed one of my heaviest textbooks. And I slammed it down onto the Grool.

"Die!" I shouted. "Please! Die!"

I raised the book high. Pounded the Grool with it.

Again. Again.

I pounded hard enough to kill *anything*.

Finally, I stopped. Gasping for breath, my arms aching, I stared down at what I'd done.

Yuck. What a mess.

Brown and pink shreds of Grool littered my desk.

I had smashed it to pieces.

"Yes!" I cried breathlessly. "Yes!"

Finally! I had finally destroyed the evil creature!

"Yes!" I cried again.

But the cry stuck in my throat.

As the pink and brown shreds started to move, I stared down in horror — and began to shake all over.

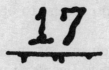

17

"This can't be happening," I whispered.

But it was.

The pieces — the shreds of Grool — they were sliding across the desktop. Slithering. Rolling together.

Coming back together.

Forming a brown ball. A sponge.

It didn't take long. A minute at the most.

And now the Grool stared up at me again. And it vibrated so hard that my desk actually began to rock.

Its cruel snicker cut through my shocked silence.

Heh, heh, heh.

"Shut up! Shut up!" I screamed.

But it snickered even louder.

Frantic, I grabbed a dirty sock from the clothes hamper. I used it to pick up the Grool. And then I hurled the thing back into the cage.

Heh, heh, heh.

With a cry, I threw myself face down on my bed and covered my ears. "Will I have this bad luck for the rest of my life? Is there *anything* I can do?"

I was so frightened. So angry. So confused.

I couldn't even pretend to be my usual cheery self.

When Aunt Louise took me and Daniel out to an ice-cream parlor, I couldn't even finish a small butterscotch sundae. Usually, I'm good for a triple decker.

But how could I ever be happy again? I was stuck with the Grool — forever.

"Wake up, Kat! Wake up!" A frantic voice whispered in my ear.

I slowly raised my head off the pillow. "Huh?"

Daniel was waving his bookbag back and forth about an inch above my head. "Get that away!" I shouted, grabbing for it.

"Hey, I'm only trying to help you," he replied, snatching the pack away. "You're going to be late for school. You'd better get moving!"

He ran out of the room.

I tore the covers off and raced to the closet. I slipped on my Save the Earth sweatshirt and purple flowered leggings. Then I remembered.

"Daniel, you little dweeb!" I bellowed. "We have no school today! There's a teachers' conference!"

He peeked back into my room.

"Got you!" he gloated.

I hurled a pillow at his head and hit him in the face. A nice shot.

"You're a bad sport," he said, laughing. "Carlo's coming over after breakfast. We can play *Mega Monster Warriors*."

I slammed the door in his face.

Daniel's stupid tricks usually don't bother me too much.

And a day off from school always puts me in a great mood.

But how could I enjoy myself? I just kept wondering what bad thing was going to happen next.

What bad luck would the evil Grool bring today?

After breakfast, I hung around on the back porch, reading a magazine. And trying to ignore Daniel's and Carlo's shrieks and wild laughter as they played computer games.

I really missed Killer. He usually sits next to me when I read.

After about an hour, I got bored. I decided to go up to my room and work on my social studies assignment.

I had to write an essay for Mrs. Vanderhoff. *My Family and What They Mean to Me*.

But I kept thinking about the Grool and how it was totally *ruining* my family.

So far, all I had written was: "I'm Kat Merton and my family means an awful lot to me."

Not exactly grade-A material. And the paper was due tomorrow morning.

I decided to take a break. I went to the kitchen and poured myself a glass of chocolate milk and grabbed a handful of oatmeal cookies.

On my way back upstairs, I peeked into the den. Things seemed very quiet in there.

I didn't see Carlo. Only Daniel, playing *Underwater Adventure Quest*.

"Where is Carlo?" I asked.

"Um," Daniel replied, his eyes glued to the submarines and torpedoes flashing across the computer screen.

"Was my question too hard for you?" I asked sarcastically. "I'll go slower now. Where . . . is . . . Carlo?"

"Home," he mumbled.

"Did he get mad because you sank more enemy submarines than he did?" I joked.

Daniel didn't answer.

I headed upstairs to my room. I set down my milk and cookies. I couldn't help but glance at the gerbil cage.

It wasn't what I saw that made a prickle of fear run down my back. It was what I *didn't* see.

The cage stood empty.

The Grool was gone.

Escaped.

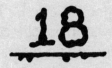

18

How had it escaped? The Grool had never even *tried* to get out of its cage before.

In fact, the stupid sponge never seemed very interested in going *anywhere*.

Why did it disappear now? And where did it go?

And what kind of trouble was it planning to make?

It couldn't get very far, I told myself. It had no legs.

I started to call to Daniel. But my throat choked with panic.

I frantically started to search for the Grool. I slid on my stomach under the bed. Not there.

I pulled everything out of my closet. I opened dresser drawers. No sign of it.

I checked every inch of the room. I even called out to it: "Here Grool, here Grool."

No. No way. The creature was gone.

The words from the *Encyclopedia of the Weird*

suddenly flashed into my mind: "Anyone who gives the Grool away will DIE within one day."

"Daniel!" I shrieked. "Daniel!" I tore downstairs and into the TV room. I shook him so hard, he dropped his computer mouse.

"The Grool is gone!" I cried. "It escaped!"

Daniel turned away from the computer screen. "Excuse me? What do you mean — gone?"

"It's gone! The cage is empty!" I wailed.

Daniel scrunched up his face, thinking hard. "I know where it is," he said. "Carlo."

"Huh?" I cried. "How could you? How could you let Carlo take it?"

"I didn't *let* him!" Daniel snapped. "He must have grabbed it when he left. Carlo thinks it's all a big joke. He said there's no way a little sponge can do anything bad."

"What a jerk!" I sputtered. "Maybe we should let him keep the Grool. It would teach him a lesson — a real nasty lesson!"

"Kat, we can't!" Daniel exclaimed. "He's my best friend. We have to get the Grool back from him — before something terrible happens!"

Daniel and I pulled our jackets out of the hall closet. Then we ran out to the garage. We jumped on our bikes and pedaled furiously down Maple Lane.

"Where do you think he went?" I shouted.

"Let's try the school playground," Daniel suggested. "There's always a bunch of kids there."

74

"Yeah, and Carlo's a big show-off," I exclaimed. "He probably went straight to the playground to show off the Grool."

"He is *not* a show-off," Daniel protested.

"Is too!" I argued. Pedaling furiously, I shot way ahead of Daniel.

I made it to Chestnut Street a few minutes later. "Only two more blocks!" I called breathlessly. I slowed down so that Daniel could catch up.

I turned the corner.

"Oh, no!" I screamed.

I squeezed on the brakes. Stopped short.

Who was that lying in the middle of the street?

Was it Carlo?

Yes!

Carlo. Sprawled on his stomach. His arms and legs stretched over the pavement.

"We're too late!" Daniel cried. "We're too late!"

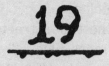

19

Our bikes crashed to the ground as Daniel and I leaped off them. We bent over Carlo, calling his name.

"Ohhhh, wow." Carlo let out a low moan. He clutched his right leg.

"Carlo!" I yelled breathlessly. "What is it? What happened? Are you okay?"

Carlo bent his leg carefully and winced. "My knee *really* hurts. I twisted it when I fell off my bike."

I looked up and saw his bike, on its side under a tree.

"How did it happen?" Daniel asked weakly. My brother hates the sight of blood.

"Some of the older kids wanted to race me," Carlo groaned. "I didn't really want to race them — but they dared me."

He sat up, still rubbing his knee. "Man, I was *flying*! Then, well, I hit some gravel — and skidded into a tree. Those kids all thought it was a riot. They just rode off and left me."

"Daniel, help me get him up," I instructed. We put our arms around Carlo and guided him over to the curb.

Then we just sat there, staring at Carlo's mangled bicycle. The handlebars looked like a giant metal pretzel.

"You know what?" Carlo finally said. "I didn't even see that stupid tree until I was right on top of it."

Daniel poked me. I knew he was thinking what I was thinking.

The Grool strikes again.

We had to get the Grool back.

"Carlo, where is the Grool?" I asked.

"Right there in my bike basket." He pointed.

I reached over the tangled handlebars and felt around the basket with my hand.

And felt again.

Nothing in the basket. Completely empty.

"Carlo, give me a break," I complained. "There's no Grool in there. Where is it?" My voice got high and shrill. I could feel the panic sweeping over me.

"Huh? It's *got* to be in there!" Carlo declared. "That's where I stuck it. I was going to take it right home."

"Oh, sure, Carlo," I snapped. "Like you weren't

going to bring it to the playground and show it off?"

Carlo hung his head. "Well, maybe for a couple of minutes."

"Great! Just great!" I fumed. "Because of you, the Grool is missing."

Daniel leaned close to me, his face pale with fear. "We've got to find the Grool, Kat," he whispered. "Remember what the encyclopedia said. If you don't find it in a day, you'll *die!*"

"I remember," I replied with a shudder. "But how are we ever going to find it now? Where can it be?"

20

"I don't even know where to start looking." I sighed.

"Maybe it fell out of the basket when I hit the tree," Carlo suggested. "Maybe it rolled somewhere around here."

Daniel tugged on my sleeve. "Come on," he urged. "Let's start looking."

Carlo stood up. "I'd better get home," he said. He limped away. Luckily, his house was on the next block.

Daniel and I hunted all over the block. In doorways, underneath cars, in flower beds — anywhere the Grool might have rolled.

No luck.

As we were about to give up, I spotted a sewer grating a few feet away from Carlo's bike. Could the Grool have tumbled down there?

Daniel saw the sewer, too. "Kat? I'll bet it rolled

down into the sewer! It's down there. I know it is!"

I dropped to the pavement. On my stomach. I peered into the darkness through the grating.

"It's way too dark to see anything," I reported. "Somebody will have to go down there."

"Uh . . . somebody? Maybe . . . maybe I could go," my brother offered in a shaky voice.

Daniel acts really brave. But I know he's afraid of a lot of things. Like dark sewers.

He'd freak out down in the sewer.

"No. I'll do it," I said. "The Grool knows me better."

We lifted off the heavy grate. I felt around with my sneaker. It slid against a narrow ladder built into the side of the sewer.

"I guess this is the only way down," I said softly. "Here I go."

Slowly, I lowered myself into the dark wet hole. The ladder rungs were wet and slippery. The walls were thick with sewer slime.

"This place really *stinks!*" I called up. "I can't believe I'm doing this."

Squishhhhh!

As I reached the sewer floor, my sneaker landed on something wet and oozy.

"Gross!" I screamed, pulling my foot back up.

"Are you okay?" Daniel called from above. He sounded ten miles away.

"Yeah," I shouted back. "I think I stepped in a pile of slime. Wow, it's really dark down here."

I carefully touched my feet down again, and gripped the ladder tightly with one hand — afraid I would never find my way back if I let go.

It's too dark, I realized. I'll never find the Grool down here.

Then I heard it.

Whoa-ahhh. Whoa-ahhhh.

Breathing!

Whoa-ahhh. Whoa-ahhhh.

The Grool! But where?

I held my breath and stood completely still. I concentrated really hard, trying to figure out exactly where in the inky blackness the breathing came from.

Whoa-ahhh. Whoa-ahhhh.

Somewhere to my right?

I knew I had to walk over there and snatch the Grool. But I was afraid to let go of the ladder. Finally, I decided to count my steps there, find the Grool — then count the same number of steps back to the ladder.

I swallowed hard and let go of the ladder. I stepped into the blackness and started counting.

"One . . . two . . . three . . . four . . ."

The breathing sounded a little closer.

"Five . . . six . . ."

I stopped. I listened hard.

"Huh?" I cried to myself. "What's that scratch-ing sound?"

Then I saw the eyes.

Not the Grool's small, round eyes.

Big, bright eyes. Several pairs of them.

All glowing at me in the dark.

21

The scratching grew louder. The eyes stared up at me.

Yellow eyes. Glowing in the darkness.

I heard a creature scrabble over the floor. Felt something warm and furry brush against my leg.

Were they raccoons? Rats?

I didn't want to know.

Another one brushed against me. They were all starting to scrape around on the sewer floor. They were growing restless.

I forced myself to breathe.

Turned.

And started to run.

Get me out of here! I thought. Get me out of here before they attack!

My sneakers slid over the damp, slimy floor.

"Please let me find my way out of here," I prayed as I stumbled through the darkness.

"Oww!"

My knee slammed into something hard.

I cried out and reached for something to lean on.

And caught hold of the ladder.

"Yes! Yes!" I cried happily.

Ignoring my throbbing knee, I scrambled up the slimy rungs. Up, up, up toward the light.

"Daniel — help me out!" I cried.

Daniel leaned down and grabbed my hands. He helped pull me out of that awful hole.

I fell on to the pavement and nearly sobbed with relief.

Daniel dropped down next to me. "Did you get it?" he asked eagerly. "Did you find it?"

I wiped my sludge-covered hands on my jeans. "No," I told him. "No Grool."

"*I* should have gone down there," he declared. "I definitely would have found it."

"You definitely would have been terrified!" I replied angrily. "There were animals down there. Rats, maybe. Dozens of them."

"Yeah. Sure," he said, rolling his eyes. He sighed. "*Now* what do we do?" He kicked a pebble across the street.

I sighed. "Don't worry — we'll find the Grool."

"But how?" he cried. "We can't even find Killer. We'll never find a little sponge."

I had never seen Daniel this upset. "Daniel, the police will find Killer. I know they will," I said softly.

"We must have missed the sponge," he said,

ignoring my words. "We have to check everywhere again."

We started to search again. In the street. In the grass. Behind hedges. Under trees.

Carlo appeared as we were about to give up. He was walking fine. He examined his mangled bike. Then he helped us with our search.

The afternoon sun was settling behind the trees. The air felt cooler. Evening was approaching.

I sank down on the sidewalk, feeling totally hopeless.

The warning in the encyclopedia kept running through my mind. Was it possible? Could it be true? If we didn't find the Grool, would my life really be over by tomorrow?

"There it is!"

Daniel's excited shout interrupted my frightening thoughts.

"There it is!" my brother cried happily. "I see it! I see the Grool!"

22

Daniel took off, running full speed.

"Way to go!" My heart pounding, I leaped up from the sidewalk. "You are the most awesome brother in the entire universe!"

I was so excited and happy, I threw my arms around Carlo. "He saved my life!" I shouted. "He saved my life!"

"Hey — give me a break!" Carlo cried, squirming away.

I hurried after Daniel. I watched him bend down to pick up something. Something small and round and brown.

But a gust of wind rolled the Grool away from him.

"Hey —!" he cried out. He stumbled after it. The wind blew it out of his reach again.

"Got you!" Daniel cried, pouncing on it.

"Bring it here!" I yelled.

"Oh, wow," he murmured. His face fell. "Sorry about that. It's not the Grool."

I grabbed the thing from his hands. "No, it's not," I whispered sadly.

Not the Grool. Only a brown paper bag, all wadded up in a ball.

Daniel hurled the paper bag to the ground and stomped on it.

My stomach lurched. I really felt sick.

Time is running out, I thought. And we have no idea where the Grool might be.

A tear came to my eye, and I blinked it away quickly. I didn't want Daniel and Carlo to see how scared I was.

The panic rose in my chest. Would I really die if we didn't find that evil creature?

I suddenly pictured Mom and Dad sitting around crying and missing me. I pictured Aunt Louise wailing, "It's all my fault. I didn't believe her."

I imagined Daniel walking to school all alone.

I gazed down at my brother, who slumped sadly on the curb with Carlo.

And I had a truly terrifying idea. Maybe the Grool *wasn't* lost.

Maybe the creepy little creature had decided to *hide*.

To hide from me.

So it could perform its most evil trick of all.

Hide for twenty-four hours so that I'd have the ultimate bad luck.

Death!

Carlo startled me by jumping to his feet. His dark eyes glowed excitedly. "I — I have an idea!" he cried.

"An idea?" I demanded. "What kind of idea?"

He smiled at me and grabbed my arm. "Come on. Hurry. I think I know where the Grool might be!"

23

"You know those guys who raced me?" Carlo asked, tugging me forward along the street. "The ones who hang out at the playground?"

"Yeah. What about them?" I asked.

"I'll bet one of them picked up the Grool. I kind of remember —"

Daniel didn't even wait for Carlo to finish the sentence. "Let's go!" he shouted. He sprang onto his bike and raced off toward the playground.

I picked up my bike and started pedaling after my brother. Carlo ran behind us, calling, "Wait up! Wait up!"

We pedaled to the playground and walked our bikes to the baseball field. That's where the older kids usually hang out.

"There they are," Carlo said. He pointed to a group of boys taking turns batting and fielding balls.

"Carlo," Daniel whispered nervously. "Those

guys are really big. They look like they're in high school."

I spotted two older boys standing on the side of the baseball field. Their heads were bent, and they were staring at something in the taller boy's hands.

Something small and round and brown.

The Grool!

I ran up to them. "Hey, how's it going?" I said in my friendliest voice. "I know this sounds dumb, but you've got my favorite sponge. Can I have it back?"

The tall boy narrowed his eyes at me. He was kind of good-looking, with bright green eyes, and straight blond hair down over his shoulders.

"Your favorite sponge?" he repeated. He grinned. "Sorry. You're mistaken. This is *my* favorite sponge."

"No. Really," I insisted. "It fell off that kid's bike." I pointed to Carlo. He and Daniel stood watching from a distance. "I really need it."

"Can you prove it's yours?" the boy demanded. He rolled it around in his hand. "I don't see your name on it."

I narrowed my eyes and gave him my meanest glare. "You'd better give it back to me," I threatened. "Because it's not really a sponge. It's evil. It brings bad luck to anyone who has it."

"Oooh, I'm really scared," he teased. "Maybe

it's bad luck for you — because you're not getting it back!"

He waved the Grool in front of my face, then called to his friend, "Hey, Dave. Catch!"

He tossed the Grool to Dave. "Here," he snickered. "Catch some bad luck!"

"Hey, give me that!" I leaped for the Grool. But the sponge sailed high over my head.

Back and forth they threw the Grool, laughing, keeping it high over my head, out of my reach.

They were having fun. I wasn't.

After ten minutes of their stupid keep-away game, I gave up.

Fine, I thought. Let them play with the Grool.

They would soon find out that it didn't play fair, I thought nastily.

As I backed off, I shouted at the two older boys, "You'll be sorry."

The blond guy shrugged his shoulders, laughed, and hurried off to take his turn at bat. He made a big show of tucking the sponge into his back pocket — where he knew I couldn't get it.

He stepped to the plate, crouched in a batter's stance . . .

Thwock!

The very first pitch beaned the guy in the head.

His eyes rolled around wildly. He wobbled, then sank to the ground. He collapsed in a heap and didn't move.

"Help!" the other boys were shouting. "Somebody — help!"

The Grool had done its work. The bad luck had struck again!

"Is he okay?" Daniel asked. "Is he —?"

I didn't answer. I saw the Grool roll out of the boy's back pocket and onto the ground.

I darted forward and dove for the evil sponge.

But my hands closed around dry grass.

Dave, the blond boy's friend, snatched the Grool before I could reach it.

"Go chase it!" he cried. He heaved the little creature high into the sky.

24

I made a desperate grab. But Dave was much taller than me. He caught the Grool easily.

"Here. Take it," he said. He tossed it at me. Then he hurried over to check on his friend.

The blond boy was sitting up now, rubbing his head. "I'm okay," he kept repeating. "Really. I'm okay. What hit me?"

Daniel and I hurried to our bikes. Carlo came running after us. I tossed the Grool into my bike basket.

The sponge creature pulsed so violently that the basket shook as I rode. Its body changed from red to black, red to black, changing in time to its horrible breathing.

Ba-boom. Ba-boom.

It snickered with joy.

Heh, heh, heh.

It acted so pleased with itself. So happy it had knocked the blond boy out.

"You're disgusting!" I shouted. "I'm taking you home and locking you in that cage!"

I pedaled rapidly, standing up for an extra boost of speed. Home, I thought. Get me home.

I zoomed down Oak Street, hunching over the bike with my head down. Faster, faster I pedaled.

The wind whipped my hair into my eyes.

I heard Daniel calling out from behind me.

But I was riding too fast. The wind rushed past me. I couldn't make out Daniel's words.

I heard him call out again.

And then I heard the blare of a horn and the shrill squeal of brakes.

I turned around in time to see an enormous black and silver truck skidding over the street, about to crush me like a bug.

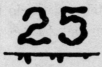

25

I squeezed my brakes hard.

The truck skidded up behind me, tires scraping the pavement, horn blaring.

My bike lurched to a stop — and I tumbled off.

Hit the pavement hard on my elbows and knees.

The bike bounced on to the curb. Toppled over.

I rolled on to the grass.

As the truck swerved away. Squealed to a stop.

Missed me by less than a foot.

I climbed shakily to my feet. And stood there on the side of the road, too terrified to move.

I turned to see the truck driver toss open the door of his cab. "What were you doing in the middle of the street?" he shouted at me. "I could have killed you! Do your parents know you're out here like this?"

Great, I thought bitterly. First this guy almost squashes me into a pancake — then he yells at me.

"Sorry!" I called.

What else could I say?

I waited for the truck driver to back up and drive away.

And all the time, I kept thinking: Bad luck forever. I'm going to have bad luck forever.

I called to Daniel and Carlo that I was okay. Then I raced down Oak Street and turned on to Maple.

Only two houses to go, I thought. I pushed down harder on the pedals.

Blam!

My front tire hit something. A broken bottle, I think.

The bike toppled on to its side, and I fell with it.

"Ow!" I cried. I'm spending a lot of time on the ground, I realized.

I examined the tire. Completely shredded.

Bad luck. Bad luck forever.

Heh, heh, heh. I heard the Grool's wicked laugh.

The sound filled me with rage. I kicked the bicycle and stubbed my toe on the metal wheel rim.

"Oww!" I yelped, grabbing my foot.

Bad luck. Bad luck forever.

With a furious cry, I grabbed the evil sponge and flung it to the ground. Then I jumped back on my bike and started to run over the Grool.

Back and forth, back and forth.

Squishing the evil creature into the ground.

"Stop it! Stop!" Daniel screamed, riding up onto

the grass. "You can't kill the Grool. You're only giving it what it wants."

I glared at my brother. I struggled to catch my breath.

"Look at it!" Daniel shouted, pointing. "The Grool is getting even more excited. You're helping it, not hurting it!"

I lowered my eyes to the Grool. It pulsed faster than before. An evil light shone from its ugly little eyes. Its blood-red body gleamed in the afternoon sun.

Heh, heh, heh.

The cruel snicker cut through the air like fingernails on a blackboard.

I grabbed my bike and wheeled it to our driveway. I let it fall on to the asphalt.

Then I ran back to the Grool, gripped it tightly in one hand, and carried it into the house.

Daniel followed close behind me. "Now what are you going to do?" he asked.

"You'll see," I said. I made my way into the kitchen.

My heart pounded. I could feel the blood racing at my temples.

I jammed the Grool into the kitchen sink drain. Then I grabbed a wooden spatula and stabbed at the Grool, shoving it deep into the pipe.

Daniel stood beside me, watching in silence.

I turned the hot water on full force. I flicked a switch next to the sink and smiled at my brother.

The garbage disposal gurgled on.

The gurgle became a whine.

The whine became a roar as the grinding teeth went to work.

"Yes!" I cried happily. "Yes!"

A few seconds later, the disposal had ground up the Grool.

"That's the end of that," I told Daniel, sighing happily. I listened to the pipes run clean. "Down the drain! Yaaay!"

Carlo came running into the kitchen. "What's happening?" he cried breathlessly. "Where's the Grool?"

I turned to Carlo, grinning. "It's gone. The Grool is gone!" I announced gleefully.

Then I heard my brother gasp.

I saw his mouth drop open as he stared down at the sink. "No, it's not." His voice was so low, I could barely hear him. "No, it's not gone," he whispered.

26

I lowered my eyes to the sink.

And realized at once what had horrified Daniel.

The hot water had started to back up.

It splashed and spurted up from the drain. As if something were pushing it with great force.

The hot water churned quickly — rolling up from the pipe below.

"I don't *believe* it!" Carlo cried.

The Grool popped up, bobbing in the churning hot water.

There it was. Still in one piece. It had turned bright purple, an angry purple. As I stared down at it in horror, it thumped wildly in the sink.

"No!" I screamed. "It's impossible! You can't be back!! You *can't!*"

I grabbed the sopping wet Grool and squeezed it as hard as I could.

A river of water ran out of the slimy thing and into the sink.

The harder I gripped, the warmer the Grool felt.

Warmer and warmer and . . .

"Ow!" I dropped it as it became scorching hot. Quickly, I ran my hands under soothing cold water.

The Grool perched on the side of the sink. It throbbed with joy, leered up at me with its creepy eyes, and let out an evil cackle.

"Daniel, Carlo," I moaned. "There has to be a way to kill this thing! There has to! Think, guys!"

But the two of them stared in silence at the throbbing Grool.

"Come on, Daniel — think!" I waved my hand in front of Daniel's face. "Help me! I'm all out of ideas."

Suddenly, his eyes came back into focus. "I've got an idea," he said quietly.

He rushed out of the kitchen. "I'll be right back," he shouted, leaving Carlo and me alone with the nasty creature.

"I hate you!" I shouted at it. But my anger seemed to make it pulse faster.

A short while later, Daniel hurried back into the room. "Maybe this will help," he announced. He set the *Encyclopedia of the Weird* on the kitchen table.

"I borrowed it from the library," he explained. "I thought we might need it."

He started to search for "Grool" in the index.

"Oh, Daniel," I sighed wearily. "We've already read everything in that book about Grools. It can't help us."

"But maybe you missed something important," Carlo insisted.

Daniel flipped through the pages of the encyclopedia. "Here's the part about killing the Grool," he said. "Let's see what it says."

He started reading: *"The Grool cannot be killed — by force or by any violent means."*

"That's it?" I demanded. "There's nothing else?"

Daniel slammed the book shut. "Nothing else," he replied sadly. "Kat, it really can't be killed. It's the most evil creature in the world and it can't be killed. Not by force. Not by violence. Not by anything."

"Not by force," I repeated, thinking hard. "Not by violence."

I stared at the throbbing, purple creature.

"Hmmmm." I couldn't help but smile.

"Kat? What's your problem?" Daniel demanded. "Are you totally losing it? Why are you smiling?"

"Because the Grool can be killed," I announced. "And I've just figured out how to do it."

"Huh?" Carlo cried. "You've really figured it out?"

101

"What are you going to do?" Daniel demanded. "You can't kill it. It always comes back to life."

I shook my head. "We'll see," I replied.

I wanted to think my plan through before I explained it to them.

Actually, it turned out to be pretty simple.

27

Much as I hated to, I picked up the throbbing Grool from the sink and held it gently in my hands.

I patted the disgusting creature tenderly on its wrinkled head. Then I sang to it sweetly:

"Lullaby and good night, little Grool, I love you. Please sleep tight, little Grool, la la la, la la la."

"Kat, I'm worried about you," Daniel groaned. "Stop it, okay? You're a little messed up. You need to lie down."

But I just kept singing as sweetly as I could.

"What is she doing?" Daniel asked Carlo. "Do you get it?"

Carlo shook his head.

I didn't pay any attention to them.

I had to concentrate.

I forced myself to stroke the Grool lovingly. I hugged the slimy thing and cuddled it in my arms — as I would a soft puppy.

I cooed in its ear:

"Little Grool, cute Grool, you are so nice, so sweet, so wonderful. I love you, Grool."

"Kat, please stop," Daniel begged. "You're upsetting me. I'm really worried about you, Kat."

"How can you pet the thing?" Carlo demanded. "It's so gross!"

"Sweet, Grool," I whispered. "So sweet." I cuddled it tenderly and stroked its wrinkled skin.

If this doesn't work, I told myself, nothing will.

"I'm going to get Mom and Dad," Daniel threatened. He started backing toward the kitchen door.

"Ssshhh." I raised a finger to my lips. Then I pointed down at the Grool cradled in my arms. "Look, guys."

The Grool's violent throbbing had slowed to a gentle pulse.

I sang some more, softly, gently, sweetly.

And we all watched in amazement as the Grool's color faded. From red to pink, and — finally — back to its ordinary dull brown color.

"Wow!" Daniel whistled.

"Keep watching," I said, hugging the Grool closely. I sang another lullaby.

The Grool let out a low sigh. I could see it shrinking, see it drying up in my arms.

Its eyes closed. The dry, brown skin covered them up.

"It — it's getting weaker, Kat," Daniel whispered excitedly.

"Keep watching," I told him. Then I cooed to

the Grool, "There, there little Grool. What a sweet Grool." I rocked it like a baby.

The Grool's breathing slowed — slowed — then stopped.

The Grool slumped lifelessly in my hand. Not a sound. Not a throb. Not a twitch.

"Now, check this out!" I announced to Daniel and Carlo.

I raised the wrinkled sponge to my face — and planted a big fat kiss on it.

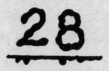

28

The two boys made disgusted faces.

But I knew what I was doing.

I lowered the Grool from my face and studied it carefully.

"*Aaaaaaaah.*" The sponge let out a long, slow sigh — and shrank into a tiny ball.

I took a deep breath and blew.

The tiny ball flew apart. Dry, brown puffs floated into the air.

I watched the feathery puffs float to the floor. Then I wiped my hands off on a towel. "All done."

"It — it's gone!" Carlo declared.

"But how?" Daniel demanded.

"Well, you helped give me the idea," I told him.

"I did?"

"Yes," I replied. "When you read that part of the encyclopedia that said the Grool can't be killed by force or violence."

I smiled. "I kept going over that in my mind. And finally, it hit me."

"What hit you?" Carlo asked.

"I knew the Grool couldn't be killed by force or violence," I explained. "But what about the opposite? I guessed that no one had ever tried being nice to it before."

Both boys stared at me in rapt silence. "That gave me the idea that being kind was the secret to destroying the Grool," I continued. "And it worked. The Grool was so evil that it couldn't stand being loved."

"Wow!" Carlo breathed.

"Excellent!" Daniel exclaimed. "I'm glad I came up with it."

"Yeah, it's great to have a genius in the family," I said sarcastically.

I reached into my back pocket and pulled out the twelve dollars my grandma had sent for my birthday. "What do you say we celebrate with ice cream?" I suggested with a grin.

"Excellent!" the two boys cried happily.

"Maybe our luck will change now," I told Daniel. "I bet we become the luckiest family on the block."

Then I heard it. That familiar, terrifying, breathing sound again.

I swung around and faced the door.

"What's that?" I cried, my heart sinking. "Do you hear it, too?"

Yes. We all heard it.

My throat felt dry. Cold chills ran down my back.

The breathing grew louder.

Closer.

"I didn't kill it," I moaned. "It's back. It's back!"

29

Daniel grabbed my hand. I could see the fear on his face.

Carlo took a step back from the door. He backed up till he bumped against the kitchen counter.

We huddled together in the kitchen, afraid to move. Afraid to go look.

"We have no choice," I choked out finally. "If it's back, we have to let it in."

I took a deep breath. My legs didn't want to carry me. They felt as if they were made of lead.

But I forced myself to the back door.

My entire body trembled as I reached for the doorknob. And yanked the door open.

"Oh!" I let out a startled cry.

Killer gazed up at me, breathing noisily, his stub of a tail wagging furiously.

"Killer!" I yelled joyfully. "You're back!" I bent down to hug him. But the dog ran past me, into the kitchen.

Daniel let out a happy cry and pulled the wiggling dog into his arms. Killer covered Daniel's face with wet licks.

"Our luck *has* changed!" I declared.

I looked outside.

Wow! Healthy green grass covered the ground. The flowers lifted their drooping heads and burst back into dazzling color as I watched.

All of the Grool's evil seemed to be disappearing.

I grabbed Killer and hugged him hard. "Killer, Killer," I crooned. "We got rid of the Grool."

"Come on," Daniel cried. "Ice-cream time!"

I set Killer back on the floor and kissed him on the head. "We'll be back soon, boy," I said.

"To the ice-cream parlor!" Daniel shouted as he dashed outside. "Race you!" he cried as he ran down the street. "The winner gets a triple-decker sundae!"

Carlo and I took off after Daniel. I pumped my legs hard and pulled out in front.

But at the last minute, Daniel pushed past me and tagged the door of the restaurant. "I won!" Daniel cried happily.

We hurried into the ice-cream parlor. "Table for three," Daniel said with a grin. The waitress seated us, handed out menus, and wiped the table with a . . . sponge!

"Yuck! Get that thing out of here!" Daniel shrieked.

The waitress didn't understand. But we all laughed — for the first time in weeks.

"Don't mind my brother," I said. "He's got a thing about sponges." He kicked me under the table, and I pinched him back hard.

The waitress rolled her eyes. Then she took our orders.

As we shoveled down our sundaes, I realized how hungry I was — and how happy I was.

The Grool was gone — forever.

We were so full that we practically rolled back home.

"Killer. Here, boy!" I pushed the back door open and stepped into the kitchen.

"Hey — Killer? Come here! Aren't you glad to see us?"

Killer didn't turn around.

He stood at the sink, growling and wagging his tail. He had his nose pressed up against the cabinet door, trying to push it open.

"All right, Killer. We had our ice cream. Now it's time for your treat," I said.

I put down a fresh bowl of dog food — and added a few small pieces of last night's turkey.

"Come on Killer. Dinnertime," I called.

He growled at the cabinet underneath the sink.

What's going on? This dog *never* walks away from a meal, I thought.

"Killer," Daniel said, "what are you doing under there? Killer?"

I bent down and petted the dog's back. "Killer, there's nothing in there. The Grool is gone."

But Killer kept growling.

"Okay, okay." I yanked the cabinet door open for the dog. "See?"

Killer shoved his head inside.

I grabbed him by the scruff of his neck and pulled him out. He carried something in his teeth.

"What is that, boy?" Daniel asked.

Killer dropped his find on the floor, then gazed up at me.

I picked it up. Hmmm. Something hard. Lumpy.

"What is it?" Daniel asked, stepping close.

I breathed a sigh of relief. "No problem. It's only a potato."

I started to hand it to Daniel.

But something sharp pricked my finger.

"Ow!" I cried, startled.

I rolled the potato over in my hand.

It felt warm. I could feel it breathing.

"Daniel, I don't like the looks of this," I murmured.

The potato had a mouth full of teeth.

Add *more*

Goosebumps

to your collection . . .
A chilling preview of
what's next from
R.L. STINE

NIGHT OF THE
LIVING DUMMY II

4

Margo came over the next afternoon. Margo is real tiny, sort of like a mini-person. She has a tiny face, and is very pretty, with bright blue eyes, and delicate features.

Her blond hair is very light and very fine. She let it grow this year. It's just about down to her tiny little waist.

She's nearly a foot shorter than me, even though we both turned twelve in February. She's very smart and very popular. But the boys like to make fun of her soft, whispery voice.

Today she was wearing a bright blue tank top tucked into white tennis shorts. "I bought the new Beatles collection," she told me as she stepped into the house. She held up a CD box.

Margo loves the Beatles. She doesn't listen to any of the new groups. In her room, she has an entire shelf of Beatles CDs and tapes. And she has Beatles posters on her walls.

We went to my room and put on the CD. Margo settled on the bed. I sprawled on the carpet across from her.

"My dad almost didn't let me come over," Margo told me, pushing her long hair behind her shoulder. "He thought he might need me to work at the restaurant."

Margo's dad owns a huge restaurant downtown called The Party House. It's not really a restaurant. It's a big, old house filled with enormous rooms where people can hold parties.

A lot of kids have birthday parties there. And there are bar mitzvahs and confirmations and wedding receptions there, too. Sometimes there are six parties going on at once!

One Beatles song ended. The next song, "Love Me Do," started up.

"I *love* this song!" Margo exclaimed. She sang along with it for a while. I tried singing with her, but I'm totally tone deaf. As my dad says, I can't carry a tune in a wheelbarrow.

"Well, I'm glad you didn't have to work today," I told Margo.

"Me, too," Margo sighed. "Dad always gives me the worst jobs. You know. Clearing tables. Or putting away dishes. Or wrapping up garbage bags. Yuck."

She started singing again — and then stopped. She sat up on the bed. "Amy, I almost forgot. Dad may have a job for you."

"Excuse me?" I replied. "Wrapping up garbage bags? I don't think so, Margo."

"No. No. Listen," Margo pleaded excitedly in her mouselike voice. "It's a good job. Dad has a bunch of birthday parties coming up. For teeny tiny kids. You know. Two-year-olds. Maybe three- or four-year-olds. And he thought you could entertain them."

"Huh?" I stared at my friend. I still didn't understand. "You mean, sing or something?"

"No. With Dennis," Margo explained. She twisted a lock of hair around in her fingers and bobbed her head in time to the music as she talked. "Dad saw you with Dennis at the sixth-grade talent night. He was really impressed."

"He was? I was terrible that night!" I replied.

"Well, Dad didn't think so. He wonders if you'd like to come to the birthday parties and put on a show with Dennis. The little kids will love it. Dad said he'd even pay you."

"Wow! That's cool!" I replied. What an exciting idea.

Then I remembered something.

I jumped to my feet, crossed the room to the chair, and held up Dennis's head. "One small problem," I groaned.

Margo let go of her hair and made a sick face. "His head? Why did you take off his head?"

"I didn't," I replied. "It fell off. Every time I use Dennis, his head falls off."

"Oh." Margo uttered a disappointed sigh. "The head looks weird all by itself. I don't think little kids would like it if it fell off."

"I don't think so," I agreed.

"It might frighten them or something," Margo said. "You know. Give them nightmares. Make them think their own head might fall off."

"Dennis is totally wrecked. Dad promised me a new dummy. But he hasn't been able to find one."

"Too bad," Margo replied. "You'd have fun performing for the kids."

We listened to more Beatles music. Then Margo had to go home.

A few minutes after she left, I heard the front door slam.

"Hey, Amy! Amy — are you home?" I heard Dad call from the living room.

"Coming!" I called. I made my way to the front of the house. Dad stood in the entryway, a long carton under his arm, a smile on his face.

He handed the carton to me. "Happy Unbirthday!" he exclaimed.

"Dad! Is it — ?" I cried. I tore open the carton. "Yes!" A new dummy!

I lifted him carefully out of the carton.

The dummy had wavy brown hair painted on top of his wooden head. I studied his face. It was kind of strange. Kind of intense. His eyes were bright blue — not faded like Dennis's. He had bright red painted lips, curved up into an eerie smile. His lower lip had a chip on one side so that it didn't quite match the other lip.

As I pulled him from the box, the dummy appeared to stare into my eyes. The eyes sparkled. The grin grew wider.

I felt a sudden chill. Why does this dummy seem to be laughing at me? I wondered.

I held him up, examining him carefully. He wore a gray, double-breasted suit over a white shirt collar. The collar was stapled to his neck. He didn't have a shirt. Instead, his wooden chest had been painted white.

Big, black leather shoes were attached to the ends of his thin, dangling legs.

"Dad — he's great!" I exclaimed.

"I found him in a pawnshop," Dad said, picking up the dummy's hand and pretending to shake hands with it. "How do you do, Slappy."

"Slappy? Is that his name?"

"That's what the man in the store said," Dad replied. He lifted Slappy's arms, examining his suit. "I don't know why he sold Slappy so cheaply. He practically *gave* the dummy away!"

I turned the dummy around and looked for the string in his back that made the mouth open and close. "He's excellent, Dad," I said. I kissed my dad on the cheek. "Thanks."

"Do you really like him?" Dad asked.

Slappy grinned up at me. His blue eyes stared into mine. He seemed to be waiting for an answer, too.

"Yes. He's awesome!" I said. "I like his serious eyes. They look so real."

"The eyes move," Dad said. "They're not painted on like Dennis's. They don't blink, but they move from side to side."

I reached my hand inside the dummy's back. "How do you make his eyes move?" I asked.

"The man showed me," Dad said. "It's not hard. First you grab the string that works the mouth."

"I've got that," I told him.

"Then you move your hand up into the dummy's head. There is a little lever up there. Do you feel it? Push on it. The eyes will move in the direction you push."

"Okay. I'll try," I said.

Slowly I moved my hand up inside the dummy's back. Through the neck. And into his head.

I stopped and let out a startled cry as my hand hit something soft.

Something soft and warm.

His brain!

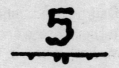

5

"Ohhh." I uttered a sick moan and jerked my hand out as fast as I could.

I could still feel the soft, warm mush on my fingers.

"Amy — what's wrong?" Dad cried.

"His — his brains — !" I choked out, feeling my stomach lurch.

"Huh? What are you *talking* about?" Dad grabbed the dummy from my hands. He turned it over and reached into the back.

I covered my mouth with both hands and watched him reach into the head. His eyes widened in surprise.

He struggled with something. Then pulled his hand out.

"Yuck!" I groaned. "What's *that?*"

Dad stared down at the mushy, green and purple and brown object in his hand. "Looks like someone left a sandwich in there!" he exclaimed.

Dad's whole face twisted in disgust. "It's all

moldy and rotten. Must have been in there for months!"

"Yuck!" I repeated, holding my nose. "It really stinks! Why would someone leave a sandwich in a dummy's head?"

"Beats me," Dad replied, shaking his head. "And it looks like there are wormholes in it!"

"Yuuuuuck!" we both cried in unison.

Dad handed Slappy back to me. Then he hurried into the kitchen to get rid of the rotted, moldy sandwich.

I heard him run the garbage disposal. Then I heard water running as he washed his hands. A few seconds later, Dad returned to the living room, drying his hands on a dish towel.

"Maybe we'd better examine Slappy closely," he suggested. "We don't want any more surprises — *do* we!"

I carried Slappy into the kitchen, and we stretched him out on the counter. Dad examined the dummy's shoes carefully. They were attached to the legs and didn't come off.

I put my finger on the dummy's chin and moved the mouth up and down. Then I checked out his wooden hands.

I unbuttoned the gray suit jacket and studied the dummy's painted shirt. Patches of the white paint had chipped and cracked. But it was okay.

"Everything looks fine, Dad," I reported.

He nodded. Then he smelled his fingers. I guess

he hadn't washed away all of the stink from the rotted sandwich.

"We'd better spray the inside of his head with disinfectant or perfume or something," Dad said.

Then, as I was buttoning up the jacket, something caught my eye.

Something yellow. A slip of paper poking up from the jacket pocket.

It's probably a sales receipt, I thought.

But when I pulled out the small square of yellow paper, I found strange writing on it. Weird words in a language I'd never seen before.

I squinted hard at the paper and slowly read the words out loud:

"Karru marri odonna loma molonu karrano."

I wonder what that means? I thought.

And then I glanced down at Slappy's face.

And saw his red lips twitch.

And saw one eye slowly close in a wink.

6

"D-d-dad!" I stuttered. "He — moved!"

"Huh?" Dad had gone back to the sink to wash his hands for a third time. "What's wrong with the dummy?"

"He moved!" I cried. "He *winked* at me!"

Dad came over to the counter, wiping his hands. "I told you, Amy — he can't blink. The eyes only move from side to side."

"No!" I insisted. "He winked. His lips twitched, and he winked."

Dad frowned and picked up the dummy head in both hands. He raised it to examine it. "Well . . . maybe the eyelids are loose," he said. "I'll see if I can tighten them up. Maybe if I take a screwdriver I can — "

Dad didn't finish his sentence.

Because the dummy swung his wooden hand up and hit Dad on the side of the head.

"Ow!" Dad cried, dropping the dummy back

onto the counter. Dad grabbed his cheek. "Hey — stop it, Amy! That hurt!"

"*Me?*" I shrieked. "I didn't do it!"

Dad glared at me, rubbing his cheek. It had turned bright red.

"The dummy did it!" I insisted. "I didn't touch him, Dad! I didn't move his hand!"

"Not funny," Dad muttered. "You know I don't like practical jokes."

I opened my mouth to answer, but no words came out. I decided I'd better just shut up.

Of course Dad wouldn't believe that the dummy had slapped him.

I didn't believe it myself.

Dad must have pulled too hard when he was examining the head. Dad jerked the hand up without realizing it.

That's how I explained it to myself.

What other explanation could there be?

I apologized to Dad. Then we washed Slappy's face with a damp sponge. We cleaned him up and sprayed disinfectant inside his head.

He was starting to look pretty good.

I thanked Dad again and hurried to my room. I set Slappy down on the chair beside Dennis. Then I phoned Margo.

"I got a new dummy," I told her excitedly. "I can perform for the kids' birthday parties. At The Party House."

"That's great, Amy!" Margo exclaimed. "Now all you need is an act."

She was right.

I needed jokes. A lot of jokes. If I was going to perform with Slappy in front of dozens of kids, I needed a long comedy act.

The next day after school, I hurried to the library. I took out every joke book I could find. I carried them home and studied them. I wrote down all the jokes I thought I could use with Slappy.

After dinner, I should have been doing my homework. Instead, I practiced with Slappy. I sat in front of the mirror and watched myself with him.

I tried hard to speak clearly but not move my lips. And I tried hard to move Slappy's mouth so that it really looked as if he were talking.

Working his mouth and moving his eyes at the same time was pretty hard. But after a while, it became easier.

I tried some knock-knock jokes with Slappy. I thought little kids might like those.

"Knock knock," I made Slappy say.

"Who's there?" I asked him, staring into his eyes as if I were really talking to him.

"Jane," Slappy said.

"Jane who?"

"Jane jer clothes. You stink!"

I practiced each joke over and over, watching

myself in the mirror. I wanted to be a really good ventriloquist. I wanted to be excellent. I wanted to be as good with Slappy as Sara is with her paints.

I practiced some more knock-knock jokes and some jokes about animals. Jokes I thought little kids would find funny.

I'll try them out on Family Sharing Night, I decided. It will make Dad happy to see how hard I'm working with Slappy. At least I know Slappy's head won't fall off.

I glanced across the room at Dennis. He looked so sad and forlorn, crumpled in the chair, his head tilted nearly sideways on his shoulders.

Then I propped Slappy up and turned back to the mirror.

"Knock knock."

"Who's there?"

"Wayne."

"Wayne who?"

"Wayne wayne, go away! Come again another day!"

On Thursday night, I was actually eager to finish dinner so that Sharing Night could begin. I couldn't wait to show my family my new act with Slappy.

We had spaghetti for dinner. I like spaghetti, but Jed always ruins it.

He's so gross. He sat across the table from me,

and he kept opening his mouth wide, showing me a mouth full of chewed-up spaghetti.

Then he'd laugh because he cracks himself up. And spaghetti sauce would run down his chin.

By the time dinner was over, Jed had spaghetti sauce smeared all over his face and all over the tablecloth around his plate.

No one seemed to notice. Mom and Dad were too busy listening to Sara brag about her grades. For a change.

Report cards were being handed out tomorrow. Sara was sure she was getting all A's.

I was sure, too. Sure I *wasn't* getting all A's!

I'd be lucky to get a C in math. I really messed up the last two tests. And I probably wasn't going to do real well in science, either. My weather balloon project fell apart, so I hadn't handed it in yet.

I finished my spaghetti and mopped up some of the leftover sauce on my plate with a chunk of bread.

When I glanced up, Jed had stuck two carrot sticks in his nose. "Amy, check this out. I'm a walrus!" he cried, grinning. He let out a few *urk urk*s and clapped his hands together like a walrus.

"Jed — stop that!" Mom cried sharply. She made a disgusted face. "Get those out of your nose."

"Make him eat them, Mom!" I cried.

Jed stuck his tongue out at me. It was orange from the spaghetti sauce.

"Look at you. You're a mess!" Mom shouted at Jed. "Go get cleaned up. Now! Hurry! Wash all that sauce off your face."

Jed groaned. But he climbed to his feet and headed to the bathroom.

"Did he eat anything? Or did he just rub it all over himself?" Dad asked, rolling his eyes. Dad had some sauce on his chin, too, but I didn't say anything.

"You interrupted me," Sara said impatiently. "I was telling you about the State Art Contest. Remember? I sent my flower painting in for that?"

"Oh, yes," Mom replied. "Have you heard from the judges?"

I didn't listen to Sara's reply. My mind wandered. I started thinking again about how bad my report card was going to be. I had to force myself to stop thinking about it.

"Uh . . . I'll clear the dishes," I announced.

I started to stand up.

But I stopped with a startled cry when I saw the short figure creep into the living room.

A dummy!

My dummy.

He was crawling across the room!

About the Author

R. L. STINE is the author of over three dozen best-selling thrillers and mysteries for young people. Recent titles for teenagers include *I Saw You That Night!*, *Call Waiting*, *Halloween Night II*, *The Dead Girlfriend*, and *The Baby-sitter III*, all published by Scholastic. He is also the author of the *Fear Street* series.

Bob lives in New York City with his wife, Jane, and fourteen-year-old son, Matt.

YOU CAN'T TEACH
AN OLD DUMMY NEW TRICKS!

Goosebumps

Amy's ventriloquist dummy,
Dennis, keeps losing his head...for real.
So Amy begs her family for a new dummy.
That's when her dad finds Slappy in a local
pawnshop. Slappy's kind of ugly, but Amy's
having fun practicing her new routine.

Then horrible things start happening.
Horrible, nasty things.
Just like what happened the first time.

NIGHT OF THE LIVING DUMMY II
Goosebumps #31
by R. L. Stine

Creeping into a bookstore near you!

RLS994

GET
Goosebumps
by R.L. Stine

❑ BAB47745-5	#23 **Return of the Mummy**	$3.50
❑ BAB48354-4	#24 **Phantom of the Auditorium**	$3.50
❑ BAB48355-2	#25 **Attack of the Mutant**	$3.50
❑ BAB48350-1	#26 **My Hairiest Adventure**	$3.50
❑ BAB48351-X	#27 **A Night in Terror Tower**	$3.50
❑ BAB48352-8	#28 **The Cuckoo Clock of Doom**	$3.50
❑ BAB48347-1	#29 **Monster Blood III**	$3.50
❑ BAB48348-X	#30 **It Came from Beneath the Sink**	$3.50
❑ BAB48349-8	#31 **The Night of the Living Dummy II**	$3.50
❑ BAB48344-7	#32 **The Barking Ghost**	$3.50
❑ BAB48345-5	#33 **The Horror at Camp Jellyjam**	$3.50
❑ BAB48346-3	#34 **Revenge of the Lawn Gnomes**	$3.50
❑ BAB48340-4	#35 **A Shocker on Shock Street**	$3.50
❑ BAB56873-6	#36 **The Haunted Mask II**	$3.50
❑ BAB56874-4	#37 **The Headless Ghost**	$3.50
❑ BAB56875-2	#38 **The Abominable Snowman of Pasadena**	$3.50

Scare me, thrill me, mail me GOOSEBUMPS Now!

Available wherever you buy books, or use this order form. Scholastic Inc., P.O. Box 7502, 2931 East McCarty Street, Jefferson City, MO 65102

Please send me the books I have checked above. I am enclosing $_____ (please add $2.00 to cover shipping and handling). Send check or money order — no cash or C.O.D.s please.

Name _____ Age _____

Address _____

City _____ State/Zip _____

Please allow four to six weeks for delivery. Offer good in the U.S. only. Sorry, mail orders are not available to residents of Canada. Prices subject to change.

GB53095